Two Hundred Thousand Years

Two Hundred Thousand Years

Stories About the Incredible Human Journey

J. G. Jung

iUniverse, Inc.
New York Lincoln Shanghai

Two Hundred Thousand Years
Stories About the Incredible Human Journey

Copyright © 2007 by Joseph G. Jung

All rights reserved. No part of this book may be used or reproduced by any means, graphic, electronic, or mechanical, including photocopying, recording, taping or by any information storage retrieval system without the written permission of the publisher except in the case of brief quotations embodied in critical articles and reviews.

iUniverse books may be ordered through booksellers or by contacting:

iUniverse
2021 Pine Lake Road, Suite 100
Lincoln, NE 68512
www.iuniverse.com
1-800-Authors (1-800-288-4677)

Because of the dynamic nature of the Internet, any Web addresses or links contained in this book may have changed since publication and may no longer be valid.

Certain characters in this work are historical figures, and certain events portrayed did take place. However, this is a work of fiction. All of the other characters, names, and events as well as all places, incidents, organizations, and dialogue in this novel are either the products of the author's imagination or are used fictitiously.

ISBN: 978-0-595-47111-9 (pbk)
ISBN: 978-0-595-70850-5 (cloth)
ISBN: 978-0-595-91391-6 (ebk)

Printed in the United States of America

I have lived and died among countless generations. Because of me, Man has become the guardian of the earth.
I am thought and I am reason.
I am Man's hard won gift of consciousness.
I have endured Man's struggles for survival in those earliest days, and will endure such struggles yet again. I have seen Man's darkest deeds and his greatest triumphs.
I have stood atop Man's greatest constructions and looked out over vast populations of thriving peoples. And I have been a witness to the merciless slaughter of countless others over meaningless beliefs. I have cried oceans of tears for the tragic loss of millions. Yet I have laughed and danced with the world at my feet.

This book is dedicated to Johan Peter Jung, my great-grandfather, who crossed the Atlantic Ocean 115 years ago, seeking opportunity and a better life.

Contents

Foreword xi

Introduction xiii

Fire 3

The Hunt 11

The House 19

Out to Sea 27

The Stone Mason 35

The Arena 49

Collapse 57

Plague 65

Oppression 73

The Radio 81

The Astronaut 89

The Dump 97

Extinction 105

Disappearing Cultures 111

Foreword

This book was written for the sole purpose of clarifying human history. It views mankind as *a* species, not *the* species. Man can be seen here as an animal who shares this isolated island of life called earth with other animals. This wonderful book avoids the common trap of losing historical meaning in a cluster of politics, specific events, and individual historical figures.

The reader will breeze through thousands of years of invention and struggle to see humanity's *big picture*. It is this *aerial view* of mankind that reveals what is truly necessary for the continued survival of his species.

Introduction

How did Man, a physical weakling, rise to dominate a planet of powerful and deadly carnivores?
Is Man responsible for past and ongoing extinctions in the animal world?
Is Man himself tumbling toward extinction?
Does Contemporary Man differ from his ancient predecessors?
Can Man's future be seen in his past?
Is Man good or evil, both or neither?
What will likely end Man's reign on earth?

Modern Man is searching for answers. He studies the contemporary and ancient world to find the answers to his questions. He digs incessantly in the earth, in an attempt to uncover his past. He has sent scientists out around the globe to find answers. As Man continues to search, he seems to find only more questions. He prays to God to understand the evils in the world and gives thanks for the good. He struggles to make sense of his existence. He can feel the weight of his impending problems. He desperately feels the need to predict his future.

Man's answers can be found anywhere and everywhere. The answers do not elude Man, but what eludes him is the ability to accept what he finds. This is a guidebook to the human experience on earth.

"Two Hundred Thousand Years" relives the human experience at different times throughout the last two hundred thousand years. The reader will travel through the great gateways of human history and witness the rise of Man. He is like no other beast upon the land, yet he is no different at all.

In those early days, there existed different types of hominid other than Man. Their populations spread over much of Africa, Asia, and Europe. They were extremely diverse in size and shape, and of course, in intellect. HomoErectus and Neanderthal were among those who walked the earth with Man, competing and coexisting, and all struggling for survival. They all used tools and some were able to harness fire, just as Man had.

Man knows of their existence through both the fossil record and through a common human memory. That memory, handed down through vast distances in time, manifests itself in stories of mythical creatures like Bigfoot or Sasquatch. In fact, Man continues to search to this very day in the most remote places on earth for his long extinct cousins. But in the end, he finds that he is the only surviving member of what was once a very large extended family.

Our story begins when at least two of Man's cousins are still present in his world. But they are soon to perish, just as all on earth, including Man, will one day pass into history. But he does not concern himself with such realities at this time. He cares only of food, defense, and reproducing his kind. He is in an ongoing battle to survive in a world that is determined to force his extinction.

Fire
Place: Africa
Time: 200,000 years ago

We are safe in a rocky overhang tonight. We are hungry and tired, but our crackling fire gives us much needed comfort. The fire means everything to us. Fire is the earth's gift to us. Its flame warms our bodies on cold nights and it protects us from predators. Lions, wolves, and the other beasts dare not approach the smell of burning wood. Long ago we learned how to make spark and heat to create fire. We cook our meat and warm our beaten bodies with the flame. Each difficult day we all yearn for the night and the warmth and power of the flame. On the nights that we cannot create a fire we feel the fear and horror of our long forgotten past. We feel the dread of the night. With nothing to protect us from beasts and cold, we are truly exposed. The ability to create fire is our greatest achievement. The chill of the night cannot penetrate our bodies. We sleep in peace and warmth and safety. None of us can image a time without fire.

We are without my child tonight. We lost him in a river today. The five of us were crossing the river this morning to find new hunting grounds and safe shelter. We hadn't had good shelter since we left the cave near the giant oak some five nights ago. We left in search of meat. The river was to my chest and the water moved quickly. I held my boy as high above my head as possible to protect him from the current. The river bed was rocky and very slippery when I lost my balance. The current sucked us beneath the surface and instantly pulled us quickly away from the others. When I finally managed to surface, I was gasping for air and struggling against the current. There was no sign of my child as the water carried me further and further from the others. As I struggled for my life, I knew he was gone. He was only three years old. When I finally came to shore, I was almost a half a day's walk downstream from the others. I headed back upstream searching the riverbank for my son. The others walked downstream looking for either one of us. When we finally met, it was clear to all of us that the boy was lost. The river had taken him. With nothing left to do, we continued on.

Our lives end suddenly, without warning, and without time to grieve. We live off the land, we grow from the land, and we return to the land. Every day we fight for survival. We protect each other when we can, but sadness is something we cannot afford. Our bodies are cold, our wounds are sore, our bellies are empty, and we are always on guard.

We can live for an untold number of years, but rarely do. Carnivores, illness, and injury always find their way to us. I am nineteen years old and the oldest of my group. To live beyond childhood is rare indeed, because most of us never survive to adulthood. And to live beyond twenty-five years is even less common.

I have no name. None of us do, but we know each other well. We can communicate with one another through sound and sight, through expression and movement, through shared memory. We remember our experiences and learn from them.

We will remember the power of the river after today. Our children can only survive by watching us and learning. They imitate us. The children who learn the fastest do better than the others.

The female in our group has been with us for years. She should be nearly twenty by now. She gave birth to the boy we lost today. She will be saddened for much longer over this loss than the rest of us. Our female has given birth once before, but the infant only lived for a few nights. We need children, but don't know how to care for them when they become ill. We are stronger than the children and can survive many illnesses, but the children cannot. We have two other males in our group. One of them has been with me my whole life, or as long as I can remember. We look out for each other and know what each other is thinking. This is good when we hunt. We are good hunters together. He is younger than I am, but I don't know how much. The other male has been with us for many seasons. We found him alone and starving when he was just a boy. He was maybe ten years old. Yet he has learned our ways quickly, is a good hunter, and never tires. His hearing is sharp and can hear things we cannot. This helps us in many ways. But my eyes are better than the rest. I can see prey and danger before the others.

Together we live. We walk great distances and forage and hunt along the way. We find good shelter when we can and stay as long as we can. We stay until we can no longer find enough food to fill our empty bellies. Then we move on. We live in a small group, as others of our kind do, for a good reason. Cooperation with other humans is difficult and often ends in killing. We keep to ourselves. We avoid other groups and keep our distance. We become aware of other groups every year or so. But they can be as dangerous to us as the carnivores.

We are different from the other animals we kill, fight, and fear. We can anticipate our needs. We understand that we need shelter and food and water. Even when are bellies are full, we know they will be empty soon enough. We know the difference between wet and dry wood. When the rains come, we hide dry wood for our fires. We know what stones to use to make a flame. We carry these with us. We hang fruit, roots, and meat in the sun to dry. Dried foods do not rot like fresh food. We carry these with us as well. We seek out certain plants to heal our wounds. We can't remember how we came to know these remedies, we just know. We can dry infected wounds and soften our pain. We know of poisons to soak the tips of our spears. We possess knowledge the other animals do not. What we lack in strength and size, we make up by working together and thinking ahead. A single man without a spear is helpless to even the smallest beast. But several men, all with spears, working together, can bring down the most dangerous of animals. Yet, someone will be injured, of course.

We have learned to hide our fear from the carnivores. One man, strong of mind and fearless, can defend himself with only a spear. It is not the man's size and strength, but his presence that matters. Some of us, the most successful among us, can force the retreat of a carnivore simply by thought and posture. We all understand the way of the beast, but for some of us it is a gift. Some can live among the beasts as equals, while others are endlessly tormented and pursued. Most of us, the rest of humankind, hide, run, defend, and fight to the death. Those who can stand with the beasts are worshiped and feared. Never stand against a man who can stand with the beasts.

I am the leader of my group. I am the strongest and the smartest. I can most always find food. The older I get the better I am at finding food. We need to live in groups of at least five to six to survive. Any less, or the loss of one, could be catastrophic. Groups of ten or more are hard to hold together because there is a lot of fighting.

We know the warmth of the sun on a cold day and feel the wonder of a star-filled sky at night. But wonder and warmth inevitably retreat as reality always sets in. We cannot escape from reality. Some nights we sleep near the safety and warmth of the fire, and other nights in the cold mud. We all dream of a place, a life, without danger, sickness, and hunger. We know it exists somewhere but we don't know how to travel there. We struggle with understanding simple problems. Our lives are hard. Each day will bring pain in some form. We live in a world that is mysterious, dangerous, and always changing. Our short lives are full of wonder and agony, but we press on. We all feel in some strange way that life will get better. We just don't know how.

Over the next 150,000 years the human condition remained much the same as it had been. There were small groups of semi-nomadic humans living off the land, from day to day, and season to season. Infant mortality was high. In fact, infant mortality would plague the human race well into modern times. In some regions infant mortality remains an incessant problem to this very day.

Man was on the verge of making his next big step. He began to migrate out of Africa to inhabit Asia and Europe in search of fertile hunting grounds, an epic journey to populate the planet. But he was unaware of populating the planet. In fact, Man knew nothing of planets. He was only aware of where he had been and as far as he could see. And he gazed at the stars in wonder.

Through painful trial and error, Man learned of the medicinal properties of plants. He made tools from stone, flint, and animal bone. With each passing generation, these tools were radically improved, making life that much easier. He also improved his weapons, allowing him to keep carnivores at a greater distance and kill wild game more quickly. As hunting became easier through the use of his new tools, Man could feed a larger number of individuals in his groups. With larger groups, Man will learn to understand his strength in numbers. With this strength, his knowledge of the world around him would accelerate rapidly. Man would no longer have to spend all his time feeding himself. He had more time to think, experiment, and invent.

The Hunt
Place: Europe
Time: 40,000 Years Ago

We wait. Crouched in the tall grass for what seems like days. We wait. There are seven of us, all males and all of the same clan. Three females and four children wait at camp and prepare for our return. Winter is approaching and the days seem short and the nights long and bitterly cold. They will get colder still as the winds and the snows approach.

The massive herds of bison can be seen in the distance. We know they come through the same wide and windswept valley at the beginning of winter. They return at the end of winter going back the other way. We are bison hunters. We work together. Together we rule the tundra. Bison provide us with most everything we have. We feast on their flesh. One kill will feed our clan for days and days. We carve their bones to make sharp and useful tools. We make daggers and arrowheads from flint and beads from bone. We make coats and shoes from the bison hides and store reserves of food. We have learned the way of the beast and together we drive off other carnivores. We never go anywhere alone. We move as group. We work together and we solve problems. We don't make the same mistakes we made on the last hunt. Life is hard and difficult, but we adapt and survive. We are the most feared of all the beasts.

We have been waiting for two days for the approaching herd. We are spread out in the same formation that worked during the last migration at the end of last winter. Two of us, the two youngest, hide atop a tall rock pile at the edge of the stream. They are a stone's throwing distance above the shallow water. This is where the bison cross the stream. The rock narrows their trail so they pass in small groups. The rest of us are in a circular formation on the other side of the stream. In front of three of us is a fallen tree for protection. We wait with three flint-tipped throwing spears each. In the tall grass in front of us we have dug deep trenches and covered them with grass. The trenches are deep enough to badly injure a bison. Our two oldest males lay waiting behind three large boulders that are well beyond the trenches. Each has a long heavy pole, made of the hardest wood we know, with very sharp and long carved wooden points. These they lay in the grass, the butt of the pole is wedged under the edge of the boulder, and they are pulled up quickly to impale a passing bison.

We wait and wait, and are rewarded for our patience. The first of the herd steps into the stream and begins to cross. As they enter the stream, we separate them from the rest of the herd behind them. The two boys on the rock pile leap up screaming and throwing handfuls of gravel and small stones into the herd. The bison in the stream suddenly rush forward to cross. The other bison in a panic stampede away from the water. Now the small group is charging toward the trenches. The lead bull collapses into the trench and we heave our flint tipped throwing spears into his back and sides. The great bison fights but cannot escape. The rest of the animals in the confusion, change direction and head for the pass near the three boulders. As they trampled past, the long wooden poles are pulled up from the grass and one caught the rib cage of a bison and snaps off in its side. It runs, snorting and panting, nearly out of sight and drops. We all rush in to finish off the bull in the trench. It is struggling for its life, but today it will lose that struggle. The loss of its life means that we will go on.

Now the work begins. We cut and drag meat for almost two and one half days. We travel back and forth from the two kill sites to our well-fortified encampment in a shallow cave at the base of the foothills. Each time we arrive at camp there is cooked meat waiting for us that the others have prepared. They have also collected berries and roots in our absence and enough firewood to burn for many days. These are good times for all of us. We are happy here.

From the mouth of our cave we can see to the horizon. The cave is well above the plain and we can see the herds stretched out in an endless bounty. We eat and sleep and laugh in the days following the kill. Warmed by the fire and bellies full, we have time to dream. We have time to think. We think of the hunt. We repair our weapons and improve their design. We stare at the night sky in wonder. We paint images on the walls of our shallow cave. These images are of the hunt and the story of our daily lives. The images dance in the flickering light of the fire at night. To us these images are magical. We carve the same images into bone and wood as charms to take on the hunt. They always bring us good fortune. We make warm coats from bison hides, and use bone and strips of hide to fasten our coats together. We make what we need to survive the long cold winters.

We will always fear carnivores, but chase them away most of the time. Sometimes we can't. We lost our oldest male to a grizzly bear in the spring, but we managed to kill the bear. We buried our leader in the same place where he was killed, with his broken spear and his charm. We removed his hide coat and shoes because they were needed by another member of our clan. We bury the dead so the scavengers won't eat them. Bison hunters are not to be eaten. We treat the dead with respect. It is the same respect we have for the bear, the bison, and the other beasts we share this land with. We learn each time we have an encounter with a bear. We have learned to run them off. Sometimes they are not chased away easily and we fight to the death. The more of us we have, the better off we are. Together, with sharpened spears, we are far more dangerous than a pack of wolves. We have learned how to keep a large carnivore at a safe distance.

Our bodies are strong. We can endure most injuries and generally heal quickly. Our strength comes from the bison. It comes from their flesh. I am nearly 6 feet tall, much taller than the others. I can lift rock, meat, or wood that weighs as much or more than I do. I can run on level ground as quickly as some larger animals. Although we are strong, and can run at great speeds, we always worry of injuries. An injury can cause a slow and painful death, or can hurt the clans' ability to kill enough bison to survive. When we are on the move, we are cautious and careful. We move slowly and always together. We move at speed only when ours lives or a badly needed kill is at stake. We move and work as one. Everyone knows what is expected of them. We share the work and we share the food. We make sure each of us have a coat and shoes to protect from winter's bite. We make containers from hide to carry and keep water. We use the fat from the bison to rub on our bodies in winter. This keeps our skin from drying and cracking which can produce painful sores.

We know what fruit grows where and when it's good to eat. We chew different plants to kill pain or reduce our hunger when we are short of food. We make rope out of plants. This is useful in carrying meat or building temporary shelters. We fish in summer when the bison herds have gone. It is more difficult than hunting for bison. Fishing takes much time and produces smaller amounts of food. But any fish we catch is nourishing and welcome. We hunt and kill most anything that moves when the bison leave. We waste nothing. We work together. We move together. Together we rule the tundra. We are bison hunters.

Man would master the art of the hunt through the last ice age which reached its height 20,000 years ago. Temperatures began to rise across the globe. As the glaciers retreated to the poles, the sea level would dramatically rise, drowning coastal areas. Inland lakes and streams, unending forests, and fertile plains replaced the ice. The world was changing, and Man would change along with it. Not only would he change, but he would lay the foundation for all the generations of Man to come. The basic structure of his future societies was born during these times.

This is also the time when the last of Man's cousins had disappeared forever. He was now the sole surviving hominid. At the same time other animals were falling into extinction, Man adapted and flourished. The way he lived and the way he died would change. He began to replace the large carnivores at the top of the food chain. His hard won knowledge of the world around him would start to pay off. He would leap over a threshold of understanding that no previous life on earth had managed to do before. He would begin to learn at a compounding rate of speed.

Until now, Man was constantly on the move. He found himself in the pattern of settling down and then having to relocate. This kept him preoccupied, constantly in search of new populations of wild game. After an area was 'hunted out', he would move on. But there were incredible changes to come. He was about to learn how to grow food, rather than just find it. And when he did, he was able live in one place for many generations. Now the efforts of a single individual could feed many, and human populations would explode.

This population explosion continues, nearly uninterrupted, to this very day. With permanent settlements and a full belly, Man would live longer and begin to solve the problems that had perpetually plagued him. Humanity was entering a technological revolution, not unlike the technological revolution of the twentieth century. But, quite frankly, advances of later times pale in comparison. His life was difficult and painful, but it was about to change in more dramatic ways than ever before, or ever since.

The House
Place: Asia Minor
Time: 7,000 years ago

Our numbers are growing every year. A new birth last night makes us a total of twenty-nine. Our five families are united, growing, thriving, and working together. Our fields of many grains stretch to the base of the woodlands. We thrash and harvest more than we can eat. We now keep more than forty goats among us. We are rich in clear water and milk, and rich in bread and meat. Our children sleep at night with full bellies. Our shelter is strong and protects us from the storms and the cold night air. But we are too many for this house. It has grown too small. The harvest is in and we will start building tomorrow. We have learned much and plan to build a long house nearly twice the length of the one we have now.

We have been living in this house for ten years. In those years we have seen flood and drought, yet we have always managed to eat and prosper. When we built this house there were only seventeen of us and my father was still alive. But the grains have spread and the goats multiplied. The river produces fish. We take milk and meat from the goats. But we take the meat only when wild game and fish cannot be found. In ten years we have had many children. All but two have survived. We are a strong and knowledgeable people.

Tomorrow we will begin building a larger house than any man has built. It will be strong and sturdy. It will comfort all twenty-nine of us as well as our goats during the storms. The women work the fields. The children tend to the goats. The men hunt, fish, and build. Today we are building. We have been preparing since the spring. We have cut and dragged timber all summer and have been removing the bark and chopping them to length. We have been doing this every evening, all of us. Today we will begin digging the holes to set the trunks upright that will support the roof. The holes we dig are as deep as a man is tall. Each trunk is placed in its hole and dirt is packed tightly around it. They are as sturdy as the trees in the woodlands. It takes us eight days to place twenty trunks for the outside walls and another three days to place the seven long trunks that support the peak of the roof. There are seven trunks on the long sides, four paces apart each. The short sides have five trunks each, four paces apart. All of the sides share the same corner trunks. The house will be twenty-eight paces on the long side and sixteen paces on the short sides. The inside walls will be as high as a man can reach. The seven center trunks are twice the height of the walls.

 The hardest task is splitting the trunks that will be raised to connect the center trunks to each other and down to the walls. We use rope we have made to hoist them into place. We carved points into the top of the trunks that pierce holes in the split trunks. This takes us twenty more days. We can afford this time because we have food stored from the fields that will feed us until spring. We will slaughter ten or twelve goats throughout the winter. We will have plenty to eat.

 Once the frame is up, we spend three more days fastening all the corners with the rope we made and used to hoist the roof supports in place. This will make the house strong and will stand firm in the wind. The roof takes time. It takes twenty days to secure the long branches to the frame. One by one, we tied the long branches together, until we had a support strong enough for the reeds. The reeds, collected from the edge of the river throughout the summer will protect the house from water. We will be dry, even in the heaviest rains. The walls of the house are made from the roof and walls of the old house. We use rock and stone to make the lower part of the walls. We cover the stones with clay we collected in baskets from the swamp near the river. This keeps insects that crawl from infesting the house. The top of the walls is made with the thick branches from the old house, woven together with tree bark. We will hang hides inside on the walls to keep the wind from blowing in through the house. There are five separate fire pits in the house, one for each family. The house takes us most of the winter to finish. It is a fine house. The biggest and best any of us have ever seen.

In spring, the other clans who live across the river and down stream, will see this house from their wooden rafts. They will be in awe of our work and will come to see how it was built. We will welcome them and slaughter a goat to celebrate the great house and their visit. You see. They gave us many baskets of grain at the end of winter some five years ago when we did not have enough to feed ourselves. They saved us from the ravages of hunger. We will feed them when they come and teach them how to build a great house like ours.

As we settle into our new house, there are a lot of activity and excitement. Hides are being hung on the walls and we all are preparing the house for the coldest part of winter. There is much to do. But we are all unaware of the approaching danger. We did not know that we were surrounded by a starving clan of hunters. They were hunters from the mountains so distant that they cannot be seen from here. Legend tells of these ancient and fearsome people that have lived in the highlands since the beginning of time itself. It is said that they live with the wolves and kill the mighty bear for food. To us, they live only in our fireside tales, late at night, with our bellies full. We speak of them with pride and awe, as if we inherited their courage, strength, and fearlessness. Tonight they are not legend. They live as starving raiders at the edge of the grain fields at the base of the woodlands. They have hunted out their rocky home and have been starving for weeks. Had we known all of this, having much more food than we can eat, we would have fed them. We would have sat around the fire with them and learned of their ways. We would have learned how one man can hunt and kill a bear as easily as we bring water back from the river. But tonight would be different.

The noise I heard sounded like a big animal approaching through the brush. I looked at my brother and his eyes told me that he thought the same. We grabbed our spears and ran from the house toward the sounds, screaming as loud as we could. Our other men were behind us, screaming as we were. We had chased away many large animals in this way. Tonight we would confront the most dangerous animal of all. As we rounded the house, I saw the starving hunters running toward us at full speed. With no time to understand what was happening, I raised my spear to throw, and was instantly flat on my back. Without but a moment's notice, I was fatally wounded and couldn't move. I could see the far end of the long wooden spear that had pierced my chest, upright and still wobbling from the impact. Beyond the raider's spear I could see the wonder of the night sky. Those countless stars that have fascinated me all of my life, all of my thirty-two tireless years, sparkled as bright as ever. The horrible sounds of the struggle were fading away, and my body was without pain. With my last breath, I felt a lifetime of worry and struggle vanish. What a wonderful life I have had. I hope my family fares well without me and one day learns of the secrets of the night sky.

This is a time in the distant past when the sun and the moon and the stars were still a mystery. Weather would come without warning, as well as invaders, disease and famine. Man knew nothing of the continents or of the depths and vastness of the oceans. He was unaware of the great advancements to come. Modern Man can look back in time, but Ancient Man could not see the future.

Man would now take his next big step as a traveler. He was no longer limited to how fast he could run, how far he could paddle, or how much he could carry. He would climb atop the wild horse and the camel to cover vast distances at great speed. These animals would remain humanity's main source of transportation over land for nearly five thousand years, well into the twentieth century. He would also invent the wheel to carry his belongings with him and quickly dispatch work in the fields. His tool making would evolve from stone and bone to shaping and casting metals.

Man would also turn from beachcomber to seafarer. He would cast aside his fears and set himself adrift in wooden boats. He first explored the waters as a coast hugging paddler, and then would thereafter harness the power of the wind. He hoisted sails made of hides above his modest vessels to capture that wind and set out into the open oceans. Wherever he went, he met others on the same journey, inhabiting new lands and distant islands, and discovering the bounty of the sea. Trade routes were established, over land and by sea. The more he traveled, the further he wanted to go. Because the further he extended his reach into the unknown, the more bounty he found. He found new raw materials and more trading partners, different tool making and building techniques, and new sources of food. Meanwhile, Man was thinking and learning.

Out to Sea
Place: The Shores of the Aegean Sea
Time: 5,000 years ago

They appeared on our shores long ago, when I was just a boy. They sailed here on a magnificent ship, its enormous size and height were like nothing any of us had ever seen before, or even imagined. It was beautifully carved and painted and was adorned with bronze and gold. Heavy cloth of spectacular color was draped over tall wooden beams which grew skyward from the boats hull. Long wooden oars protruded through holes along its sides. As they approached, we could see the sails being lowered and folded. Everyone onboard seemed to be working as one. And there must have been nearly fifty of them. We all stood in both fear and amazement as the oars were dipped into the water and the boat slowly made its way to the beach. Word spread across our village like a wildfire. In near panic the elders quickly assembled all the villages' men, with weapons in hand, and led them to the water's edge. The women and children were hurried into their homes. Although I was just a child, I managed to escape the orders of the elders, and hid atop the rocks behind the beach. From there, I witnessed the unfolding events that would shape my life and fill my dreams for the rest of my days.

I could sense the anxiety of all on the beach as they braced themselves for an attack. Yet from my stony perch, I felt no danger, just the excitement of getting a closer look at that amazing ship. A stone's throw from the beach, the ship seemed to magically stop in place. It was as if it were commanded to do so by some unseen force. Then a tall man made his way to the front of the boat. He was dressed in brilliant colors and wore gold jewelry around his waist and over his shoulders. I could see the others step aside as he walked, and bowed their heads as he passed. We could all see that this man was not feared, but respected. I could see that the fear of our elders and young men on the beach was turning into anticipation and wonder. We all saw that he was a great man.

Once standing on the bow, he spoke. We could not understand his words, but understood that he meant no harm. While he spoke, we saw others lowering a small raft into the water. The raft was no larger than a basket one man could carry. On top of the raft was what seemed to be a gift covered by a beautifully painted hide. They pushed the small raft toward the beach, yet the seafarers remained aboard their great ship. One of our young men on the beach was told to enter the water to retrieve the small raft. He was clearly afraid, but would not question the elders' order. The raft was brought ashore as the great seafarers watched quietly and patiently. The elders slowly removed the covering of a hide that was decorated in red and green and gold. Underneath were a sword and a shield unlike anything any of us had ever seen. The sword's handle was studded with polished gems of every imaginable color. The blade itself was longer than a man's leg and so heavy it required the elder to use both hands to raise it. It was completely covered with engraved images, and was so finely polished it reflected the image of the bearer. I saw the elder look to the ship's leader in amazement. He reached down to lift the shield. It was carved with the images of their people and their magical land, studded with colorful gems and gold. What craftsman could have made items of such beauty and fine detail? Their leader spoke again, gently, and raised hands as if to say, take this gift, we come in peace. The elder signaled them to come ashore. And they did.

They stayed with us for many days. We feasted and laughed late into each night and poured over every detail of their great ship. We spoke different languages, but that never hindered our festivities. When they finally departed, their ship was laden with a hundred or more large jars of grain, enough to feed a village throughout a long winter. We were left with three of their magical swords and shields, and the promise of a return visit. We now had great and powerful friends from a far away land. They would return every year, and each year our bond would become stronger.

Years passed and I became a man. I had many children, fields of grain, and many goats. My house was the finest in the village, with stone floors and painted walls. I had been chosen to lead our first expedition to the city of our great friends. We have learned how to build the same great vessels throughout my lifetime. Our friends have taught us well and given us much. We treat them as our brothers. They have given us maps on animal hides of the path our ship must take along the northern coastline and then out into the open sea. They have taught us how to use the sun to maintain our course in the open waters. Our vessel is decorated as beautifully as the first glorious ship I saw as a boy.

The ship was loaded with grain and wine in huge clay jars. It would take us a full moon to a full moon to reach our destination. We were all overcome with excitement to see their incredible city. We all have dreamed of this day for many years. The elders have all since passed into the afterlife. So we dedicated our journey in their honor. We have learned the way of the sail and I have hand picked my crew.

Our first ten days, sailing north along the coast, passed without incident. The weather was good and the sea calm. On the eleventh day we turned away from the coast, toward the setting sun, and out into the open sea. Uneasiness began to overwhelm the crew as none of us have ever left sight of land and sailed into open waters before. But we trusted our seafaring friends and their knowledge of the sea. Twelve more days passed on the open sea. The sea was as endless as I have always imaged it would be. But I saw the growing fear in the faces of my crew. Three of them had already taken ill. They all feared that we will never see land again. But I reassured them that we were noble, and that we would be greeted as heroes upon our return. So we pressed on.

Another seven days had passed, and all aboard were fearing the worst. That evening, as the sun set yet again, we still found ourselves surrounded by an endless sea. The men spoke of being lost and never again seeing their homes and families again. They talked of sea monsters and lost seafarers sailing to the edge of the earth. I comforted my men that night, as I would have a scared and lonely child. I recalled for them, that day on the beach, so long ago, when the great seafarers first arrived at our shores. I reminded them that we were chosen for this great journey, and that we were special. I urged them to believe in themselves and to sleep in peace. We would be heroes when we return home.

We awoke the next morning to the sound of gulls. Seagulls meant land. We leaped to our feet to inhale the most breathtaking sight of our lives. It was the great city. The great city of our seafaring friends, perched on a hill at the mouth of a bay. It was filled with a hundred ships as grand as ours. White stone houses, stacked one atop the other, completely covered the hillside. It was just as they told us it would be. There were people and ships and a whirlwind of activity. We quickly lowered our sails and rowed into the bay. With each ship we passed we were greeted with smiles and cheers. It was as if everyone here had been anticipating our arrival. As we made the shore, even though we had never been to this place before, we all felt like we were home.

Man was now learning how to live, not among the beasts, but among his own species. And it would prove to be one of his greatest challenges. For the first time in Man's long history, he was living in large groups. His villages had grown into cities, and those cities were capable of supporting populations in the thousands. It is in this environment that humanity would pass through the next great gateway of history.

His list of advancements during these times would be endless, as would be his list of atrocities. Governments would be formed to create laws and enforce them. This offered a degree of security to the city dweller by keeping the peace, and reducing the threat of chaos. Like the individual, the city itself would need to defend against outside invasions. This painful reality would be relearned again and again throughout history, giving rise to walled cities, paid mercenaries, and standing armies.

Man's trade routes were flourishing too. But they were creating more than just wealth. They were also creating human slavery. Slavery would be the scourge of mankind and last well into modern times. Ironically enough, as slavery grew and flourished, so did sculpture, painting, mechanical and architectural design, and general artistic expression. Man would also invent written language. He was becoming literate. He made great strides in mathematics and astronomy. But Man would never stop gazing at the stars in wonder.

Man created money to ease the age-old difficulty of trading goods for goods, being especially useful on trading routes and in urban areas. Currency initially appeared in the form of metals that were widely accepted as valuable, like bronze, silver, and gold. Those metals would eventually be struck into coins. Unlike cumbersome goods and resources, money could be more easily carried, hidden and hoarded. Great concentrations of wealth would then find its way into the hands of a very few. And these concentrations of wealth would create a great chiasm within human populations, forever separating the powerful and wealthy few from the rest of humanity. The way the powerful lived during these times would rival even modern times in luxury, comfort, and extravagance.

The Stone Mason
Place: An Island in the Mediterranean
Time: 4,000 years ago

Our island is the jewel of the civilized world. Surrounded by an emerald sea, the beauty of this land is without equal. We have become wealthy beyond our wildest dreams and possess all the knowledge of mankind. Our friends and trading partners are the most powerful people the world has ever known. The colossal Egyptian empire lies to the south, Troy to the north, and Mesopotamia to the east. Beyond the reaches of our trading routes the barbarians and dim-witted savages live like animals. We, on the other hand, live like gods.

 The long column of slaves stretches well beyond the horizon as it meanders like a giant snake to the base of the construction site. The familiar snaps of the foreman's whip echoes through the hillside. They are carrying rough-cut limestone from our quarry two days' ride by horse from here. The governor owns some five hundred slaves and has granted me use of more than two hundred and fifty of them to move the limestone to the building site. Today they will bring ten blocks that are eight cubits squared and four blocks twelve cubits squared. Also, coming is sixteen circular blocks to be used for the base of the front columns.

 We are behind schedule, having taken more than fifty-five days to complete the foundation. I am the master stonecutter for the construction of the largest palace ever to have been built here. I am sitting on the finished foundation we carved from pure white limestone. This site is perched high above the town, and I can see for miles in every direction. We have the finest tools and use the most advanced techniques to construct the governor's palace. The structure can be seen by all who enter our harbor. It will be a wonder of mankind when completed. The foundation measures two hundred and forty-five cubits across its face and one hundred sixty-five cubits deep. It will have two levels and measure some 60 cubits in height at its main gate.

We cut and shape stone every day, from the break of dawn until the sun sets. Most of us have worked together all of our lives. My father was a stone-cutter too, as was my grandfather. In the old days my grandfather was paid in food, wine, and leftover stone. He used that stone to build the house that our family still lives in. I, on the other hand, am paid in silver. I use the silver to buy fish near the harbor in the evening and bread from the bakers in town. I also use it to buy cloth to make my fine garments and materials to make my tools. I am rich. My family eats well and is respected here. No one here, of the common people anyway, dare to challenge me with a dispute of any kind. I always have the governor's ear because I am the best stonemason of my generation.

My name is Emul. I am forty years old and have worked on all the finest projects in our port city. As a young man, I watched my father oversee the construction of the harbor. Any trader or dignitary who enters the harbor is amazed at the harbors' beauty. He was the best stone-cutter of his time. I watched and learned from him, for he taught me well. My father spent his final years sailing to the cities of our trading partners to instruct their masons on how to build harbors of their own. He died years ago when the vessel he was traveling on sunk in a terrible storm. Our previous governor had a memorial stone placed in his honor at the entrance to the harbor. Everyone who enters sees my father's name written in stone. It is a great honor for my family.

I can see another slave being punished with the whip from here. We have had many problems with these slaves since our project began. Every time we have had these problems it slows us down. So far, we have put seven slaves to death for attempting to escape, and another nine because of broken bones. Two others have been crushed to death by falling stone in the quarry. Although I am not responsible for the quarry or transport operation, the delays still reflect poorly on me. I have a great name and I am ultimately responsible for the success of this project. The governor has been understanding and has granted me ten more slaves. He is a great man.

It will be sixty days before we receive the marble from our fleet to be used for the interior of the palace. This should give us plenty of time to erect the outer walls. We already have a stock pile of cedar tree trunks to support the roof. The clay tiles for the roof are already being made. We have a completion date of next spring, exactly one full year from the start of this project. There has been much to organize.

The sun is disappearing on the horizon as the stones from the quarry are being unloaded in the order they will be taken to the foundation tomorrow morning. My crew and I sit here long after the sky turns dark. We drink our wine and discuss the events of the day and our tasks that we need to complete tomorrow. There is much laughter here tonight, for we have completed the foundation. It is square and level. It is the largest foundation ever built. I'm sure. In fact, an entire town could probably rest right here where we sit.

I always speak confidentially with my friend Parma. Even though I oversee the palace construction, I speak to Parma as an equal. I often seek his advice. The other masons dare not challenge him for this reason. We have worked together all of our lives. His father was a mason like mine was. Tonight we talk of our days together as children. The wine makes our stories grow each time they're told. He recalls the time when we were no more than 15 years old. We were out at the end of the newly built harbor, watching the merchant ships arrive. There is an area in the harbor that is only to be used for the governor's vessel. We, of course, knew this. The harbor was crowded that day, but the governor's dock the only one that was vacant. As one of the vessels entered, because the harbor was so crowded, it slowed to a stop. It was within shouting range of where Parma and I stood. We were both thinking the same thought and began to laugh uncontrollably. We have always been able to read each others thoughts. We collected ourselves and shouted at the incoming vessel. 'Go there! Go there!' We shouted over and over, while pointing at the governor's dock. We heard the commands of the captain as the oars began to maneuver the vessel into the governor's empty dock. We watched as the vessel slid into the open space. Even before the vessel had stopped, at least a dozen of the governor's guard went running toward the vessel with swords drawn. At that very moment we both felt the dread of what we had done. We ran as fast as we could in a panic, and stayed away from the harbor for many days until that vessel had departed. As time passed, we would laugh harder and harder each time we retold the story. Twenty five years have passed and we still cannot control our laughter.

What a friend he has been. Our conversation quiets again, as it always does after recalling that story. He then talks about his wife with sadness, as he always does after a good laugh. She died during the birth of his third child. Parma has never healed from her passing. She was a good woman and was his closest friend. He remembers her smile and loving arms. She would sing quietly to him in the evenings and talk about their life together. Her name was Nessa and she was as beautiful a woman as either of us had ever seen. It has been seven years since her death. She is buried behind Parma's house. I know he talks to her every night. He has taken another wife, but it is not the same. I can see the sadness in his eyes when we speak of her.

Well, the jar of wine is empty, and Parma and I head home. It has been a good day and I will sleep well tonight. We look out over the foundation gleaming in the moonlight, and I feel much pride. It is amazing, even to us, that we are able to build such things. This palace should stand for a thousand years. Some will say it was built by the hand of God himself. Tomorrow we will begin to raise the front wall, and we expect a visit from the governor. I will arrive tomorrow much earlier than usual. The governor will expect a thorough report on our progress, and I expect that he will be pleased.

The world was moving faster and faster with each passing century, or at least parts of the world. Improvements in trade and commerce, language and art, construction and social sophistication were as great as any time in human history. Advancements in the production of food were fueling it all. But much of the world was no further along than it had been one hundred thousand years before. Populations on the fringes of civilization were still surviving as hunter-gatherers. This would remain this way until the twenty first century. Yet even the most advanced societies of this time were lacking knowledge that modern Man takes for granted. He would have a lot to learn.

He could not understand diseases or what caused them. The stars, sun, and moon were beyond his comprehension, as were wind and weather. He could not explain tidal waves or earthquakes, volcanoes or typhoons. Thunder and lightning were caused by angry gods punishing Man for his deeds or weaknesses. Man believed that unseen and mysterious forces were controlling things in his world that he could not explain.

He prayed to these gods for forgiveness, and built statues in their likeness and temples to honor their powers. He made bloody sacrifices seeking the good graces of his gods. He began to express belief in an after life. He created codes of conduct, dictated by his gods, which would insure order and prosperity on earth, and favor in the afterlife. He would seek the approval of his gods in every aspect of his life. There were gods of the sun and wind and water, and of fertility, wealth, and war.

Those who controlled access to the gods controlled the powerless and powerful alike. Two thousand years would pass before science and knowledge would reveal the true forces at work in Man's world.

The Sacrifice
Place: Central Asia
Time: 3,000 years ago

It is the night of the full moon and all of the nobles are gathering outside our holy temple. The temple is the center of our lives. It is here where we secure the favor of the gods and insure our prosperity. There are at least one hundred of us here tonight, and we are all nobility. The women are banned from such important ceremonies because they are not our equals, they serve us. The laborers and slaves are nothing more than oxen in human form. They are mentally inferior to us. They provide us with labor in the fields and sacrificial blood when we have none other to offer.

Dressed in red and gold robes with offerings in hand, the priests walk in a slow procession toward the temple. Following the priests are their wards, three for each of the seven priests. They are all dressed in black with their faces shrouded and carrying silver bowls. Raging torches line the temple mount. It is a cool and clear night, it is a special night, it is like a dream. The priests are chanting prayers to the deafening drumbeat and our hearts are racing in anticipation of tonight's great sacrifice. We have created a great and wealthy society and have magical powers. Our gods speak to us through the priests. Our priests can read the stars and the angry seas. They understand the hidden meaning of events and can predict the future.

Tonight we will sacrifice a young girl on our holy altar.

It is a special occasion. She is the daughter of our greatest enemy from across the majestic peaks. She is untouched, as her father had raised her to be a future queen. He has no sons. We captured her in a raid in retaliation for the burning of our western fields by her father's guard. We have kept her in seclusion and prepared her for this great day. The high priests have bathed her every dawn and every dusk for a month, and she has been anointed with fragrant oils from the east. We have adorned her with the finest jewels in our kingdom. She has eaten specially prepared foods of the finest quality. Every seventh day, at the break of dawn, she has been brought to the entrance of the temple. Members of the council come to kneel at her feet offering their gifts of gold and cloth. These gifts will insure the perpetuation of the temple and honor the temple priests. She is the greatest sacrifice our people have ever offered to our gods. This is a great day for us.

As night falls, the procession starts from the priests' quarters where the girl has been held in seclusion. At the head of the procession is the bearer of the sacrificial dagger. The dagger was made long ago by our ancestors for occasions like this. It rests on a pillow of black satin and draped in gold beads. The priest raises the sacred knife high above his head so that everyone present can see. Behind him are the two elder priests walking side by side and chanting our ancient hymns. In a long procession, with our torches in hand, we all slowly make our way to the broad white steps of the temple. The young girl is being carried on a bed of white linen by our highest ranking guards. She has been heavily sedated and is calm and quiet.

The procession enters the main hall of the temple which is a place of unspeakable beauty. The stone walls are carved with magical images painted in brilliant colors. Raging bronze torches fill the hall with an eery flickering light. We encircle the altar as the young girl is placed on the granite table at its center. All that can be heard is the heavy breathing of the guards preparing the girl for the sacrifice. She lays in a near slumber, as the priests gently bind her arms with soft white cloth to the large bronze rings on either side of the granite slab. As the high priest stands over the young girl, he places his hands on her, and lowers his head to speak.

His words fill our hearts with pride and emotion. He speaks of our lost warriors and the greatness of our people. He recalls the sacrifice of the great war a generation ago, and the city we have rebuilt from the ruins. What a great and determined people we are, anointed by the gods, and gifted in so many ways. We have overcome calamities and suffering brought on by our enemies. But now with the blessing of our gods we are empowered. We have taken control of the trade routes on land and sea. We have enslaved our enemies and have grown rich and prosperous. The priest speaks to the girl, but she cannot understand his words, and is barely conscious. He speaks to her gently as if she is his own beloved daughter. He tells her that she is not to be held for ransom, for we do not need the remaining riches of her father's kingdom. We have riches of our own. We prepare her today for our gods. He tells her that she is the most valuable gift that we can offer our gods. He praises her and honors her people for providing us with such an important gift.

We can hear only the crackle of the torches as the high priest raises his sacred dagger. He stands motionless in what seems like eternity, gripping the weapon with both hands, reciting words in a near whisper. Our bodies are trembling with anticipation. With one great thrust the priest heaves the dagger into the young girl's chest. As the sound of the blow echoes through the hall, we see the girl's body contorting in shock from the blow. We stand in silence as we wait for the girl to pass quietly into the afterlife. The wards quickly scurry to the granite slab to collect the sacrificial blood in their silver bowls. The blood will be used to anoint all who are present. It is an incredibly moving ceremony to witness. Everyone here today is truly blessed and will show their gratitude to the high priests for months to come with gifts of all sorts. The girl's body will be cleaned and wrapped in white linen. Tomorrow at the break of dawn we will incinerate her in a pyre at the towns' center. But for now, we celebrate our good fortune and future prosperity.

Servants arrive with large vessels filled to the brim with our finest wine. We will talk and laugh late into the night. We will drink and relish in our power and wonder of the godly favors that may come our way.

Man's growing cities expanded into surrounding areas and grew into city-states. Neighboring city-states collided, both in trade and war, eventually evolving into nations. Nations collided as well. Some weaker nations submitted to stronger ones, while other nations exhausted themselves in struggles for supremacy or survival. War, trade, riches, and slavery flourished. Nations walked a fine line between prosperity and total loss. Total loss could mean that the inhabitants of an entire nation could be cast into slavery. And slavery was, as it always would be, shameless and brutal.

The collision of peoples and merging of nations would produce Man's most infamous creation. The Empire. The Empire would ensure that wealth and power would be consolidated on a scale never seen before, or since. A single individual could control the fate of thousands, even millions of people, over vast geographic areas. The Empire would be responsible for creating Mans most enduring achievements and most shameful atrocities. Empires would come and go throughout Man's history, but once he had tasted Empire, he would forever be seduced by its powers.

These ancient empires would erect humanities' most colossal structures. Enormous palaces, temples, and tombs were appearing all across the globe. From the Egyptian pyramids to the Great Wall of China, and from the Acropolis in Greece to the great Aqueducts of the Roman world, these were testaments to his ingenuity.

Built of granite and limestone, sandstone and marble, they would stand for thousands of years.

More important than his temples and pyramids were the cities themselves. The cities needed to be supplied with the essentials, like clean water, fresh food, and basic security. Those in power who provided those necessities most successfully would stay in power for long periods of time. But that was not enough. They also needed a spectacle, or ways to divert the population's attention away from their dangerous and often hopeless existence. Man's next great invention, the Arena, would give them that diversion. The arena offered entertainment to the people on a grand scale, and in a controlled environment. Similar to modern stadiums, they serve as pressure valves to release tension in the volatile and combustible atmosphere of the city. They help to diffuse Mans instinctual aggression, and are essential for maintaining order in the city.

The Arena
Place: The Roman Empire
Time: 1,800 Years Ago

The city is bustling with activity tonight. The clap of hoofs on the cobblestone, the noisy congestion of the crowded streets, the peddlers and pigeons, the raging torches and flapping banners, all tell me I'm home. The sights and sounds are like nowhere I've ever been. Everyone here seems to be unaware of everyone else, moving at a hurried pace, always late to be somewhere. People pass one another without so much as a look. Except for the street people, they watch everyone and everything, constantly in search of their next opportunity. You have to keep your wits about you here and be on guard, always. Rome is a wonderfully fascinating place, but dangerous nonetheless. Sometimes you feel like you are alone in the middle of a crowd, like no one sees you. But beware, because there are many who watch your every move. They will steal the sandals right off your feet before you know what has happened. They are masters at their trade. Like all in Rome, they are the best of the best. No matter what your trade, Rome attracts the best. So if you desire Rome, you had better be the best at what you do, or she will devour you. She will leave no trace that you were ever there. Beware the traveler seeking riches, for you may be the riches that Rome herself seeks.

Entering the city just before the break of dawn is like entering a strange and mysterious world, especially during the games. Everyone has come to the center of the city to see the great spectacle at the Colosseum. Rich and poor, servants and freemen, senators and foreign dignitaries alike, all flood the streets. Normally the guard would clear the vagrants and beggars from the night streets. But for the next twenty days, the streets will be clogged with tents, carts and supplies, and people from all over the empire. They camp in the streets for miles upon miles surrounding the Colosseum.

Merchants line the corridors that meander through the shadows of Rome's majestic buildings. Some are residents that can be seen on any given day, while others are in Rome for the first time. They sell everything from elixirs and charms, to garments and weapons, and food and wine. It is a sight that one can see nowhere else, but Rome. There is the familiar bone-chilling sound of the emperor's guard, stomping in a thunderous march through the maze of activity. The crowd parts, allowing Rome's most visible sign of order to navigate its way to the Colosseum. These are the streets of Rome, where order and chaos live together. The rules of law and the law of the street live side by side. It is exactly as I remember.

I was released from my employment as a construction worker nearly two months ago. It has taken me this long to travel back home. I have walked more than three hundred miles from the outskirts of Turin to the streets of Rome. I have been away for four years, and have learned much about road building and bridges from my service in Turin. Now I know how these streets beneath my feet were made. I know how Rome herself rose from the seven hills. When

I left Rome all those years ago, it was all a wonder to me. But now I know of the masons and quarries, and of the surveyors and engineers. I know of cranes and winches, levels and squares. I know of the labor and toil of worker, soldier, and slave alike. I know of thousands of laborers working together, working as one. I have felt the whip of the foreman and have seen the undisciplined pay with their lives. As I make my way to the center of the city, I think of Rome's eternal beauty and her ancient past. Her colossal statues seem to come alive, as if they could leap from their pedestals to defend the empire themselves. The city's towering marble columns inspire all who pass. She is the greatest achievement of mankind. The closer I get to the Colosseum, the more crowded it becomes. I remember my father telling me as a child never to walk the streets of Rome alone. Rome is not new to me.

Just as the top of the Colosseum was coming into view I heard a fight break out behind me. I turned to see what was happening and was knocked to the ground by a man rushing past me. Within seconds, I was being trampled by the crowd, my purse ripped from my waist, and I was fighting for my life. Somehow the mobs' anger had turned on me. They punched and kicked me and tore my clothes to shreds. I screamed in protest and fought back in vain. Before long, I was battered and bloody, lying unconscious in the street. When I awoke, my hands were bound behind my back, and I was being dragged off by soldiers. I screamed to protest just long enough to be beaten into unconsciousness once again. When I regained consciousness, I realized where they had taken me. I was beneath the Colosseum, caged behind iron bars, and there were many others there too. A hundred pairs of dark and sunken eyes met mine. At that moment I understood what they already knew. Today would be the last day of my life. How can this be? The guards came for us, taking four or five at a time. Each time they came I protested, and demanded to be released. They only laughed in response. The roar of the crowd and the thunder of their stomping feet could barely muffle the screams of those dying in the sand above us. I had never been to the games before, although I now remember bragging about having been there.

Eventually, after several hours of lying in the filth and the stench, I was taken away with five others. We were herded onto a wooden platform. I could tell from the rope and pulleys that we were on an elevator, and would be lifted up to the floor of the Colosseum. I knew this from my years building wide boulevards and mighty bridges. I understood the mechanics of it all. Yet I couldn't understand how my life was being swept away in an instant. The platform began to move. I could hear the wood creaking and the ropes stretching as we began to rise. The guards heaved six swords onto the platform. I wasted no time in grabbing the largest one. We had no time to think or to speak to each other, we knew what was waiting for us. We knew that we would need to fight for our lives now. How or why we managed to find ourselves here was unimportant. Those thoughts seemed as far away as my childhood, and my mother's voice. From the time I entered the city last night to this very moment, everything has changed. I am no longer a citizen of Rome. I am her captive. My only thoughts are of death and dying. I have no name, no history, and no future.

The trap door opened, releasing the deafening sound of the crowd and the blinding sunlight. I rushed through the door and ran as hard as I could away from the others, until the sun was at my back. I watched as the other five were butchered where they stood, cut into pieces for the pleasure of the crowd. There were mutilated bodies strewn everywhere, along with abandoned weapons. The crowd reacted with a gasp as the gladiators turned to pursue me. I was the only one left standing among the bodies. The three gladiators, bloody swords in hand, were all panting from exhaustion as they surrounded me. I raised my sword, and with all my might, I hurled it at one of them. To my surprise, it struck him dead square in the chest blade first, and made a loud clank. The gladiator fell to the ground and the crowd fell silent. I had killed him. If I could kill him, I could kill another. I bolted across the arena with the gladiators in pursuit. I was much faster then they were, I had no armor to weigh me down. I picked up two more swords. They surrounded me again, but kept a greater distance and approached me more cautiously. The crowd was on their feet urging me to kill the other two. I heaved a sword at the closest one, only to have it bounce off his shoulder. He charged me and I threw the second sword, slicing through his neck, nearly severing his head from his neck. He dropped dead. The crowd screamed their approval as I darted across the arena again. This time I picked up a spear and a sword. If I could kill two of them, maybe I could kill three. And if I could kill three, maybe I could go home.

I gripped my weapons as if I were the gladiator. My fear of the arena had passed. I did not care about my lost freedom or the tip of my opponent's sword. I charged him and killed him. And I took great pleasure in the affectionate roar of the mob. I strutted around his body, my sword stretched high in the air, to incite the crowd further. There would be more gladiators to come, and I welcomed each and every one of them. I survived for nearly two hours, taking eleven souls with me. It was as if my entire life was spent here, in the blood soaked sand of the Colosseum. By the time the last gladiator plunged his blade into my chest, I had forgotten who I was, where I came from, and how I had come to this place.

Some empires would last more than a thousand years. During those times humanity would experience long periods of uninterrupted advancements and growth. Each new discovery would lead to another discovery, and then another. The longer the empire lasted, the greater the number of achievements and the grander their scale. Thinkers and inventors, visionaries and scholars, could work within the protective confines of Empire. Their wants and needs provided, their personal security guaranteed, they could spend their days in thought and debate with other like-minded individuals. Like the bison hunter of prehistory, warm and dry, well fed and safe in his cave, the thinker had time to think. In this environment, Mans growing number of inventions would soar. Although critical knowledge will continue to elude him, his inquisitiveness never faltered.

Man struggled his way through rising and falling empires. And when empires fell, advances would stall. Much was lost in the carnage of the passing of the Ancient world. From medicine, surgical techniques, and construction technologies of the Egyptians, to the advanced road, water, and military systems of Rome, to the political and social ideas of Greece, it would take centuries to relearn what was lost. With each calamity, humanity would take a step back. The greater the calamity, the greater the loss.

To survive in densely populated cities, an individual needed only to do one thing well. He could be a baker or blacksmith, a tinker or tax collector, a fisherman or a weaver. The individual would become specialized, only performing a single task. This is beneficial to the society and the individual so long as that individual can continue to depend on the society to provide him with his other basic needs. But when empires fall and cities are pillaged, individuals find that they are incapable of providing themselves with their own basic needs. This scenario is repeated all too often throughout history.

Fresh food and clean water are essential for life itself, while shelter and basic personal security are essential for order. When nations fail to provide these basics for their population, regardless of the circumstance, chaos will ensue. Whether it is a starving hoard living on the fringes of an empire, or a suppressed and exhausted general population, either will instinctually kill for food, water, and safety. Centuries of advancements in culture and the human condition inevitably disappear within hours of the removal of food and water. Man is capable of great things, so long as he is well fed, sheltered, and safe.

Collapse
Place: The Italian Peninsula
Time: 1,600 years ago

She had been the glory of mankind for more than a thousand years, my beloved Rome. We possessed more knowledge than all who had come before us. Our monuments stood as a testament to the power and glory of Rome, and our achievements would never be matched. Our libraries were filled with volumes of our unprecedented wealth of knowledge. Fifty generations had conspired to document this knowledge of everything in our world. Politics and mathematics, astronomy and medicine, weapons and warfare, engineering and philosophy, all would be cast to the wind. I was to witness the loss of it all. It would be a loss so great that we would only be remembered for our ignorance. We had been entrusted with Man's most precious possessions, and we let it slip away. Rome could not continue to endure such calamities without ultimately succumbing to disorder.

I am Marconius, and was fifty-seven years old at the time, and as healthy as I was at twenty. I was the Administrator of Antiquities and Records Building. I held that position since my father died more than twenty-five years before. My family had held important positions for four generations. Mine was one of the most prestigious positions in all of Rome. I dined with the senate, and had an audience with the emperor himself more than once. I was considered Rome's most loyal citizen and was entrusted with overseeing her greatest possessions. I understood more than anyone what is at stake. I knew intimately what was contained within the Hall of Records, more so than any man alive. What was so meticulously kept and cataloged, was in fact, the entirety of Man's history as collected over the centuries. There were jewels and documents, treaties and artifacts, and all the collective knowledge of the contemporary world. I feared that all would be consumed in the days that followed, and we would be cast into the darkness. We would retreat to our dismal past of ignorance and suffering.

Citizens had been fleeing the city for weeks. A city whose population easily exceeding one million permanent residents, was now reduced by two-thirds. The citizens still in the city, were too poor, too weak, or too frightened to flee. They were all that was left to defend the city. It wouldn't be much of a fight. The nearest Roman legion was still a month away and already depleted by relentless attacks in Germania. I feared that they would arrive too late, or never at all. Our five main aqueducts carrying water into the city had all been compromised and our food supply was cut off. In their panic, Rome's own citizens committed unspeakable crimes against each other. The city had already been pillaged, and had fallen into chaos even before the barbarians had begun their siege.

The barbarians began making camp on the other side of the river and their numbers were growing by the day. There were a hundred thoudand of them. And they were anxious and determined to avenge centuries of Roman rule. We could hear them howling and chanting at night. They were constantly taunting us. When the wind blew from the south, we could smell them. I had spent the previous three or four days hiding Rome's most important documents and relics. If I was to perish in the catastrophic disaster to come, no one would know of what I had hidden and where I had hidden it. If that building was destroyed, these treasures would be lost forever.

The first wave crossed the river at dawn. I could see the invasion from the roof of the Antiquities Building. Some ten thousand Roman citizens met them at the river's edge. These were citizens of Rome, not soldiers. They wielded clubs, swords, and spears. None were wearing armor of any sort. They collided with the invaders on the muddy banks. By midday, all of the Roman citizens had been dispatched, as continuous waves of barbarians flooded the edge of the city. They hacked their way through the streets, devouring everything in their path. Just several hundred feet from where I was were the markets. The starving barbarians stormed through the tents and shops, eating what they could and destroying the rest. Lifeless and dismembered bodies were strewn as far as I could see. As each additional wave entered the city and spread out, I knew it would be only a matter of time before they broke down the main doors of the Antiquities Building. I waited on the roof for more than two days. I had several jars of wine and many loafs of bread. The only way I could survive was if they only looted the building and moved on. If they decided to burn it to the ground, surely the roof would collapse, taking me along with it. Entering the building would require the use of a battering ram, as hammers and axes could not possibly penetrate the main gate. This was Rome's most impenetrable structure.

The invaders were not trained warriors, but bands of half-clothed and half-starved barbarians from the very edge of civilization. The Roman legion was still three weeks away. But when the legion arrived, the invaders would stand no chance of survival. They would be pursued and butchered as they themselves had done. They would certainly take flight upon news of the impending arrival of the legion. I needed to stay alive until then.

On the evening of the second day, I could see fires throughout the city. The screaming of the fallen Romans on the first day had given way to the laughter and celebration of the invaders. Dancing and drunkenness filled the streets. There were makeshift executions for the pleasure of the mob. On the morning of the forth day, they turned their attention to the main gate of the Antiquities Building. They built a fire at the gate in an attempt to weaken it, and kept it burning for two days. I remember as a child when the main gate was being fashioned by Roman craftsmen. It was made of iron so thick that it had to be hoisted to its hinges by the largest lever in Rome. Its hinges, of which there were three per gate, were each as large as a man.

On the evening of the sixth day, the mob used a battering ram made from a large timber they had stripped from an adjacent building. All day, over and over they tried to enter the building, pounding the main gate. But the gate held fast. The more they tried, the more determined they became. They circled the building looking for weaknesses in its structure, but there were none. Well, almost none. Somehow, the following morning, they had infiltrated through the water system. Even though they had not breached the main gate, they were inside the building. Within minutes the main gate was open. They poured in, and over the course of the day, they emptied the building of its valuable contents. By night fall, the interior was ablaze. The heat it produced was so great I could hardly stand on the roof. It burned all night. I no longer worried about the fate of Rome, but of my fate. My fear was more than I could bare. I wept like a child that night, fearing that I would never leave there alive. But to my surprise, the roof held.

By the time the Roman legion reached the city, the barbarians had already left. Rome was all but completely destroyed. The fire beneath me had burned itself out. About half of the legion remained in the city to reestablish order. The other half divided into smaller parties which set out to track down and kill the fleeing barbarians. Once the barbarians were caught, they were crucified by the tens of thousands along Rome's main avenues. Their bodies were left hanging for months, until they were eaten by scavengers, or just disintegrated completely.

As for the Antiquities and Records Building, only the shell remained. Everything inside was lost. The gold and silver artifacts were carried away, and the papyrus and animal skin documents were completely destroyed. All that survived was the memory of what was once here.

As for me, I would spend the last two years of my life struggling to survive among the ruins of the decimated city. As for Rome, she would never fully recover, and before long, would herself vanish into history.

Man harnessed fire in the long forgotten past, warming his body and cooking his kills. He built shelters to insulate himself from the weather, and fashioned weapons to protect himself from carnivores. He hunted in packs to bring down large game, and settled down to grow his own food. He built boats to sail the seas and rode the horse to fly over the land. He carved solid rock to build his cities, and became wealthy beyond his wildest dreams.

He saw his empires collapse and learned to defend himself from himself. But now he would face a new threat. A threat brought about by his rising numbers and wretched living conditions in densely populated areas. The new enemy is invisible to his eyes. It has no smell and makes no sound. It travels from one individual to another without notice. It is of the microscopic world, of which Man is ignorant.

The weight of his sins bore down on him. As he once prayed to his gods to calm a violent storm, he now prays to know the source of the scourge that he will not understand for centuries. He is helpless and turns to his gods for relief, but none will be forthcoming.

Millions are dying a grueling death and he is powerless to stop it. He lashes out at his brethren, committing unspeakable atrocities, in an attempt to punish any possible culprits. He tries in vain to end the suffering, but all he tries fails. Economies collapse from absence of labor. Crop failures and food shortages ensue, leading to widespread starvation.

Plague
Place: Europe
Time: 600 years ago

'God has forsaken us, the bishop declared. We must mend our evil ways, for we are being punished for our sins. We have fallen from God's grace.' Those words rang true for all who have made it this far. We stared at each other with darkened eyes, frightened and drained of hope. The stench of death is inescapable. In a last attempt to fend off the evil that has ravaged our town, we have barricaded ourselves within the walls of the bishops' abbey.

There are eight of us here including the bishop. We have kept fires burning at all four entrances for nearly a month. As the last weaken victims from our town below have attempted to enter, they are driven off with stones and lances. Many have died right there just outside the wall surrounding the abbey. Their corpses are growing in numbers with each passing day. They are our friends, relatives, and our neighbors. There is nothing more we can do but try to save ourselves. We are stricken with grief and guilt.

The abbey sits on top of a grassy hill overlooking the town, less than an hour walk away from the cathedral. Although it does not lie in the town's center, the abbey has always been the center of life for all who live here. The bishop has resided here for nearly thirty years, and draws believers for hundreds of miles. Our town has taken great pride in our religious importance and has a great deal of affection for the Bishop and the church. Bishop Merche has witnessed hundreds of births and baptisms, anointed the dying, and married our young couples. He has presided over our religious celebrations with all the pageantry that would be found in Rome. Pilgrims from far away villages have always come here for our Easter celebration. Our town during Easter is a magical place. The streets crowded with believers, praying and weeping, watched the Bishop's procession make its way from the abbey to the cathedral. There were always thousands in attendance. I am afraid there will be no Easter celebration this year, nor in any future year. I have been reminded of Hell all of my life, but deep down I felt that it was a mythical place. Many of us felt the same way. That was our sin. And for our sin, Hell itself has arrived at our door. We know now that it is not a mythical place, and we fear that we will be witnesses to the end of the world.

The plague arrived here almost two months ago, but we were unaware of what was happening until it was too late. A peasant farmer had brought his elderly mother to the steps of the cathedral on a sunny Sunday morning. She was very ill, coughing uncontrollably, and in a great deal of pain. Her body was covered with infected sores and boils. The farmer had brought her here to find a physician to cure her. Two others in their house had already died of the same illness. Shortly after arriving she was ushered off to a nearby house where our physician could attend to her. By the following evening the woman had passed away. She was given her last rights and buried in the community cemetery on the outskirts of town. For days afterward many of the townspeople came to the physician to learn more of her illness. It was such a horrible disease that we all wanted to know of its source.

Within a week, there were outbreaks all over our town. Within a month, nearly the entire town was infected and people were dying every day. No one here had ever known of a crisis like this. The bishop announced that there would be no more funerals held and that the bodies of the victims needed to be incinerated. For days on end there were pyres burning throughout the town and into the countryside. Many residents filled their wagons with as much as they would carry and left town. Others stayed to assist with the disposal of the dead and tend to the dying. Before long, there was no one willing or well enough to remove the dead from their homes. Women, children, and the elderly, unable to remove their dead loved ones from their homes, let them decay where they fell. Others died in the streets, in a final effort to find help. Hundreds of corpses lay throughout the town. Once home to more than four thousand residents, our town is nearly vacant. There are but a few hundred or so left, either wandering aimlessly through the streets, or congregating at the gates of the abbey.

There were eight of us in the abbey nearly a month ago when the bishop ordered that no one will pass through its gates. We are all still here, for none of us have taken ill.

We continue to feed the fires at the gates that separate us from the others outside the walls. With each passing day we hear less and less activity from the world outside. It has grown quiet.

That silence was broken by the thunder of many horsemen in the distance. The sound of horses in a full gallop grew louder and louder. Several of us ascended the staircase leading to the top of the wall surrounding the abbey. Some fifteen to twenty riders were headed toward us. We saw that there was a standard bearer riding the lead horse, and the standard is that of the King. We quickly summoned the Bishop, who ordered that the gate be opened. Just as the gate is opened, the riders stormed into the compound, each leaping over the smoldering bonfire at its base. As the last horseman entered, we slammed the gate closed behind them. We led them into the main hall of the abbey, and felt hopeful that the King had sent his emissaries to rescue the bishop. The bishop will undoubtedly request that we be taken away as well. But it was not to be.

The emissary read from a manuscript in an official manner, without a hint of emotion. He told us that an evil plague had blanketed the kingdom and that no village or town has escaped its wrath. Hundreds of thousands of our brothers and sisters have already died a gruesome death and as many more have taken ill. Drastic measures are needed and that all travel is forbidden throughout the land. Upon pain of death, no man will travel the King's roads until further notice, that all trade has been suspended. He instructed us to burn corpses and clothing, anything that had touched an infected person.

The King's horsemen rapidly mounted their horses, and hurried off. They were gone as quickly as they had come. As they vanished into the distance, we stood in silence and disbelief. We turned and looked to bishop Merche. He slowly sat down and lowered his head into his hands. We waited quietly and patiently as he prayed. One by one, we knelt down beside him and joined him in prayer. The Bishop led us in prayer for the rest of the afternoon. The room became dark as the sun disappeared beyond the horizon. I felt the presence of God with us and an enormous weight being lifted from my heart, as I think the others did as well. We all seemed to breathe a sigh of relief as we lifted our heads. There was no sound in the room but our breathing and the sound of birds chirping outside in the distance. We examined each others faces in the fading light when the Bishop spoke. He told us that there would be much to do in the morning, and that God has entrusted us to embrace our suffering brothers below. We would need to open the gates of the abbey and organize the survivors tomorrow. We will bury the dead, have faith in our Lord, and carry on. "God Bless you" he said.

Human populations were not all developing at the same rate, as isolated and smaller groups were generally slower to advance. Two thousand years after the Egyptians built the Great Pyramids, populations in the Americas were just beginning the construction of their own. Many populations lived much as they did some 20,000 years before, hunting and gathering and scratching a living from what the wilderness would provide. While others, at precisely the same point in time, were relishing a life of trade and technology, law, leisure, and abundance.

Oftentimes, these very different populations were unaware of each others existence. They were separated by impassable mountain ranges, endless desert, and the vast, open expanses of the worlds oceans. But when they met, neither would soon forget the other. History tells of countless meetings of this kind, with nearly all ending in a bloodshed. Flint tipped arrows fought against armor and cannon. Trained horsemen ran down barefooted warriors, and mighty ships met with dugout canoes.

Such was the case with the European discovery of the Americas. The Europeans, equipped with the technology to understand latitude and longitude, could now pinpoint their position in open waters. Combine this with a new ship design that allowed them to sail into the wind, and the sailors lost their fear of becoming lost at sea. And with that new confidence, they set out to chart the oceans. In the process, they stumbled upon the Americas, two connected continents stretching from pole to pole. The human populations already there had been mostly isolated from the rest of humanity for many thousands of years. There were millions of people already inhabiting the Americas at this time, as there were millions in Europe. But those in Europe had inherited thousands of years of Mediterranean advancement and technology that was nonexistent in the Americas. The populations in America had not domesticated the horse or the camel, because there were no camels and no horses in the Americas 500 years ago. They had long ago gone extinct, leaving Man to travel overland on foot.

The clash of populations separated by thousands of years of knowledge, has been relatively common throughout history, but never on such a colossal scale. Never had the prize been so great. The fate of two of the planet's continents lay in the balance, and the natural resources of which were intact and endless. Lured by those resources, the European populations would flood the Americas and lay claim to all as their own.

Oppression
Place: European Colony in the Caribbean
Time: 450 years ago

17 July Year of our Lord 1562
Marietta,
It pains me to have to send this letter to you. I was anxious to see you in September, but that will not be. If our current schedule is met, I will arrive in Lisbon in December. My ship ran aground on the treacherous reefs a short distance from port here last month. The ship was badly damaged, but we have been working tirelessly, with limited supplies, to repair the damage to the hull. When it became apparent that we would be delayed for two months, I took the liberty of sending this letter on the next outgoing vessel. I hope this letter finds you well and in the care and grace of our Lord.

We were heavily laden with silver and gold bullion, along with more than a ton of gems and other interesting items. We left on schedule in heavy seas and no sooner were we under way that we hit the reef. Because of our unusually heavy load we listed to port and capsized in an instant. The official report penned by the Governor, placed responsibility for the incident with the dock master, who improperly loaded the ship. This voyage in particular has been wrought with problems. It has been the most difficult of the many I have carried out for the Crown and my love, Marietta.

From Lisbon to Elmina back in March, we were driven dangerously close to shore by a violent storm. Many of the containers of textiles were soaked with sea water and destroyed. This problem was no doubt caused by poorly built containers at the factory in Lisbon. Upon arriving in Elmina, we discovered that an unknown illness had swept through the ranks of the slaves we purchased for the journey to Hispaniola. My crew had to be quarantined aboard to protect them from contracting the illness. I went ashore and personally accepted only the fittest of slaves for the long journey across the Atlantic. I did not choose well. Within days at sea my cargo was dying by the dozen. We hadn't noticed the dead at first until the stench from the hold became unbearable enough to investigate. Seventeen had perished in the first few days. As we discarded the corpses overboard, I could think only of the impending financial catastrophe. Normally we calculate 10% loss on the journey from Elmina to Hispaniola, but on this voyage we would lose a full three quarters of our cargo, not to mention the impact on the crew when they realized that we are being escorted by hundreds of sharks. The sharks appeared when the first body went overboard and stayed with us across the entire width of the Atlantic.

We bring the African slaves to the West Indies because they live longer on less food than the natives here. The natives here are physically weak and fragile and die almost instantly with the slightest beating. That is the entire purpose of the Africans, they live for many years. But now they are dying too.

Our adventures ashore were far more dangerous than my two previous trips, having had lost eight crew members in skirmishes with the savage natives. Smelting gold and silver into bars has become more dangerous. The natives are taking greater risks to disrupt our efforts, the natives that are left that is. When the first Conquistadors arrived, some forty or fifty years ago, it is said that the natives numbered in the millions. They are fairly scarce in the coastal areas now. Many can be found further inland, if you wish to tire yourself hunting these wretched people. They are weak and stupid and die easily. It is quite surprising that they are able to disrupt our activities at all. Yet they had delayed our return trip by at least 10 days. Eight of our men were lost in the fighting, but we sent more than 500 of these miserable people to their deaths. If they were of the same character as we, or even if they were remotely capable of accepting the Lord, we might treat them with less severity. The individuals who are willing to accept our Lord are converted and spared, but they are very few. The rest are dying from their inherited weakness, used for labor, or dispatched outright. But as it is, they are no different from a stubborn mule or obstinate swine. The earth will rejoice at their passing. And I will rejoice upon arrival in Spain and bask in the afternoon sun and recall for you my many adventures.

There is something else that will require discussion. The Governor has offered to me a gift for my loyal service of many years. He has granted me 50,000 acres on the mainland along with 1,000 slaves and the rights to sell the resources from that land to the Crown. The land has an abundance of tillable prairies to grow crops. It has rivers and lakes full of the most delicious fish, along with groves of wild fruit trees as sweet as the sweetest in Spain. The estate has a natural harbor and a sandy shoreline that meander as far as the eye can see. And with the labor of a thousand slaves, I will build a manor suitable for a king. The Governor has also granted me passage on any vessel in the royal fleet for the remainder of my years. So when my heart yearns for the paved streets of Lisbon, it is there we will go. I will have many legal duties to fulfill upon my return. I need you to notify Father Hormilion of my intentions and have him notify the Governor of Lisbon. There will be much to do.

The ship's hull is very nearly completed and she is being prepared for our return voyage. We will be continually delayed until such time as my instruments can be replaced. They and other equipment should be aboard an incoming vessel within days. I am in need of additional crew members as I have lost eight in fighting and two from illness. I expect to set sail in early October. I will not be for lack of adventure until then as I have been requested to join a contingent headed inland to find and execute a group of remaining natives responsible for the recent attacks. This may take some time. It matters only that this pristine land is rid of them. I find it noble to clear this land of such primitive savages for the good of the god-fearing people of Spain. Yet it is such exhausting work, wielding a sword of such weight for days on end. There is no real danger though, as these natives are easily dispatched. It is the loss of valuable time that is so costly. We are blessed with the strength and grace of God himself and will create a world suitable to worship him. I pray these dangers I face and efforts I make will be rewarded in heaven.

When we meet again, we will be relishing the fermented grapes from your family's vineyard. I will bring home gifts like you have never seen before. I pray that the Lord will be with you and watch over you.

Loyally Yours,
Captain Michael Hernanz

Man ruled the seas and within only two centuries he had mapped the coastline of nearly the entire planet. Soon there will be no place on earth that is unknown to him. The populations of the world share knowledge as never before. New cultures emerged as populations intermixed with one another. As oppressed and persecuted populations declined and in some cases vanished completely, the whole of humanity was growing at a tremendous rate. Cities and congested regions were supporting burgeoning populations in the millions and food production was accelerating as never before. Distant sources of food were now being shipped and consumed around the world.

In the centuries to come Man will understand much of which has escaped him so far. Science will soon solve the wonders of the night sky, but not without a fight. This new found knowledge will challenge the foundation of his social world. Old superstitions no longer satisfied his inquisitiveness as each passing generation learned more of the actual workings of the natural world. Science was now competing with the old religious order and answering questions that had previously been out of reach. With each question answered there would only be more questions. Disease and death ceased to be the work of the devil, and personal misfortune was no longer a result of a lack of faith or commitment to a religious order.

One of Man's new discoveries, the glass lense, would allow him to move beyond the limitations of his own eyes. As the horse and camel gave man their speed and strength, the lense would give Man nearly unlimited vision. He could now see the moon, planets, and the stars in great detail, and learn of gravity, galaxies, and orbits. He was finally learning of the wonders of the night sky. His new eyes also gave him the ability to peer into the microscopic world. He would learn of bacteria and viruses and molecules. An entire universe of tiny things that had been impacting his life since the beginning of time was now coming into focus. He would be the first creature on earth to see such things. There would be no aspect of Man's world that would remain unaffected by his new vision. But there were greater things to come.

Man had harnessed fire for warmth, made tools for protection, built ships to sail the seven seas, and carved solid rock to build his cities. Now he would achieve the unthinkable. He would reach into the sky, as did his gods of legend, and grasp a bolt of lightning. And in the process, the human condition took the greatest leap in all of human history. He would harness the magical power of electricity to light up his cities and power enormous machines that could do the work of a thousand men. Radio waves, powered by his newly found source of energy, allowed a single man to speak to millions of his brethren simultaneously, no matter the distance between them.

The Radio
Place: North America
Time: 70 years ago

We always looked forward to Sunday night. Even though my brother and I had to get up early for school on Mondays, we still loved Sunday night. Our parents' couldn't afford regular vacations, so Sunday night was very special to us. Our downstairs neighbors, the Wagners, almost always visited us on Sunday nights to listen to the mystery program and the president's broadcast on my parents radio. It's the only time we ever had company. My mother prepared coffee for the adults and popcorn for us. Mr. and Mrs.Wagner would bring the butter for the popcorn, and cream for the coffee. You see, Mr. Wagner worked at the grocery store down the block, so they got that stuff for free.

    I will never forget one particularly frigid night. I remember earlier that day, my mom said it was going to be the coldest night of the year. It was the dead of winter and the ice always collected on the windows. When the wind blew, it rattled the windows in the gangway, and made the back door shudder. But it didn't matter, because we lived on the second floor, and it was always warm in our flat. The heater constantly made strange noises, knocking, clunking, and hissing. Sometimes I thought it was alive, like it had a mind of its own. About two years before, my dad's boss gave him this radio. I guess the boss bought a new one and didn't need this one anymore. It was the most incredible thing any of us had ever seen. Dad would never tell us how much it was worth, but it was surely worth more than we had at the time. The Wagners always commented on how beautiful it was. We were all so proud to have it. It was really big and had a beautifully finished wooden cabinet with polished brass controls. When you turned it on, the dial lit up and turned a beautiful green color. I couldn't imagine how it worked. Voices traveling through the air and coming out of that speaker, it was like magic. There were a lot of different stations too. Some stations talked about the news, and others were just like movies without the pictures. Sunday nights were for mystery shows and the president's broadcast.

My brother and I would help my dad rearrange the living room furniture so everyone had a place to sit around the radio. We put the coffee table right in the middle, so everyone had a place to put their cups and popcorn. We always had to get three extras chairs from the kitchen for us kids. The adults got the sofa, which was fine by me, because I used to pull my chair really close to the heater to keep my feet warm. For a while it seemed like any other normal Sunday night. The popcorn was delicious and its aroma filled the room. The mystery program wasn't that good, and I could see my dad becoming impatient. It would usually go on for an hour, until eight o'clock, but that night was not going to be like any other night.

The mystery program was interrupted at about a quarter to eight. It was an important news flash. My dad hurried to the radio and turned it as loud as it would go. Everyone became quiet and leaned forward to hear every word. We all sat very still. It was something very important, though

I didn't quite understand at first. I stared into my mother's face for any sign of what it all meant, then her expression abruptly changed. I would remember the words we heard on the radio that night for the rest of my life. They would ring in my ears from time to time throughout the years when I would recall my youth. It still makes me cry thinking of the look on my mother's face that night. She has been gone now for some time, but I remember it as if it were yesterday.

'We are under attack' are the words I remember most. The voice went on to explain that we were at war, and that many had perished in the attack earlier that day. He said we were fighting an evil enemy that was intent on our destruction, and that all of us would need to make many sacrifices for the war. As the news flash ended, my dad slowly walked over to the radio and gently turned it off. He sat back down and everyone remained silent for what seemed like eternity. After a while my mother and Mrs. Wagner began to weep. I had never, up until that time, seen my parents so frightened and sad. In the weeks that followed, we would listen to the radio every evening, for hours at a time.

The radio was our connection to the outside world, and we listened intently for any bit of new information. As the war raged on our radio became more and more important. It used to be just for our enjoyment, but now it seemed as if we needed it for our survival. As more and more of our soldiers were being sent overseas to fight, just as many were coming home in coffins.

Our other neighbor's son, Michael, was drafted and shipped off to fight in the war. He was only gone for a few months before he was shot and killed. He was only eighteen years old. When his body was finally sent home, his parents had a big funeral for him. There were other soldiers there carrying his flag-draped coffin. That was the first time I had attended a military funeral, but it wouldn't be the last. But it was the sound of the bugle that sent chills down my spine. Every time I hear a bugle like that, I find myself beginning to cry. The reception after the service was strangely pleasant though. Some people were smiling and others laughing a bit. Michael's parents were being kissed and hugged, and given envelopes with money inside. Their friends told them that we live in a free country because of the sacrifice they and Michael had made.

My brother was too young to go into the army. And I am a girl, so I didn't have to go either. We watched as the world seemed to change before our very eyes. Everything seemed different from what it was before. Factories stopped making whatever it is they were making and were used by the government to make tanks and guns and parachutes. No one could buy a new car because none were being made. The food we bought at the store was rationed, meaning you could only buy a certain amount. That meant that there would be enough for everyone. Times were tough before, but they became even more difficult.

Our neighborhood planted a garden in a nearby empty lot to grow vegetables. Everyone on our street shared the work and shared the food. We called it a Victory Garden. It was the pride of our neighborhood. The fresh tomatoes were always one of my favorites. Yet, through that entire part of my life, we would always sit in front of that beautiful radio in my parents flat. When I think of my childhood, I always think of that radio.

When the bad news came, it saddened everyone. But when good news came, like it did when the war ended, we celebrated. My parents hugged and kissed, and danced together in the living room the night we heard the news. They laughed and sang for hours. My brother and I sang and laughed too. It seemed as though that voice on the radio could wash away years of sadness and worry with a single word. It wasn't too long before the soldiers began to come home. There were parades and parties and everyone was without a care in the world. The returning soldiers looked so brave and handsome in their pressed uniforms and shiny medals. I felt privileged just to say hello to a passing soldier on the street, just having spoken to them. They were like heroes to us. My gratitude for those boys has never left me.

Even though I am an old lady now, I can still remember those days as clearly as ever. My affection for that radio has not left me either. I still have it. Although it doesn't work anymore, it sits in my living room, covered with a doily, with my mother's old lamp on top.

By the start of the twentieth century Man's world was unrecognizable from just a century before. The locomotive was transporting huge quantities of food and raw materials from the interior of the continents with incredible speed. The industrial revolution was manufacturing goods at a blistering pace. The stage was now set for the population to explode. And explode it did. With food and materials racing to the burgeoning cities, wealth was being consolidated in a way not seen since classical times. That wealth paved the way for large numbers of individuals to spend their lives working on further advancements in technology, And advance they did. The automobile, fitted with a combustion engine, would carry common people across newly paved continents with the speed unknown to Kings and Monarchs just a few years before.

At the same time that the spoken word was being sent across the globe on radio waves, flying machines had taken to the air. One of Humanity's oldest and wildest dreams, the freedom of soaring through the skies with the eagle and the hawk, was now reality. Man was now airborne. There was no place on the globe that was inaccessible to him. There was no raw material that could not be extracted from Mother Earth. There was apparently no problem that could not be solved. But Man was entering a new era with new problems.

Humanity has always warred with itself. In the early days there were small battles, and as communities grew larger, so did the conflicts. As communities grew into cities and nations, those conflicts grew into war. Nations grew into Empires, and wars evolved into wide scale atrocities, genocide, and oppression. But now with instant communications from literally anywhere on the globe, nations unrecognizably intertwined in the trade of raw materials, and populations dependant on distant sources of food, war would take on a new meaning. No longer would it be clear as to what was being fought for, or what ignited a conflict. And no longer could a war be contained as before. Modern wars would now be fought globally. World war would remain with humanity, until the point in time that different populations no longer relied on each other for the necessities of life. World War would kill tens of millions of people in the twentieth century alone.

Yet the death of so many would have no impact on the population. In fact, the population throughout the globe would grow without restraint, as the world population doubled in the twentieth century. And soon it would double again. The quantities of food and raw materials needed to support Mans runaway population grows exponentially.

So technology soars around the world to find solutions to his ever growing problems. As one problem appeared to be solved, more problems emerge. And with technology unlocking the natural laws unknown to Man since time immemorial, Man decides to find more answers among the stars. His quest for knowledge is insatiable. He must see for himself that which has astonished him for hundreds of thousands of years. He sets out to build a machine to launch him off the earth and into the heavens.

The Astronaut
Place: Earth's Orbit
Time: 40 Years Ago

Outer space is an unforgiving place, black, and void of life. There is no air to breathe, no wind, no water, and no weather. No living thing exists there. Temperatures soar wildly beyond earth's atmosphere. In the shadow of the moon the temperature can dive to 200 degrees below zero, and in the path of the suns' rays, climb to 200 degrees above zero. It is an environment of extremes. The threat of solar radiation is ever present, as is mechanical failure and instant death. Space is a vacuum. The crushing pressure would instantly reduce a man to dust. An astronaut has to be entirely protected from the environment out there. His equipment and life support systems are critical to his survival. There is no room for error. A single mistake or miscalculation can end in disaster.

It had taken years of trial and error leading up to the launch. Countless rockets had exploded, and many people had lost their lives. But the ultimate goal of launching a man into space was far more important than the loss of life. Everyone involved was well aware that they were making history. The equipment was checked and rechecked for months. The astronaut reviewed the launch and re-entry procedures over and over again. Nothing could be left to chance.

The morning of the launch was clear and cool, without a breath of wind. The conditions were perfect. The astronaut had been sealed in the capsule several hours before the countdown began. Beneath the capsule, within the body of the rocket, were several thousand pounds of rocket fuel. Beneath the body of the rocket were the engine and exhaust nozzle. A catastrophic explosion was always within the realm of possibility, considering the quantity of explosives on board. As mission control began the final countdown, the astronaut lowered his head and quietly recited a prayer. He prayed for God to watch over him and protect him. He wanted to see his family again. He asked God to forgive him his sins.

Upon ignition, the engine screamed to life and spewed an enormous cloud of noxious exhaust that engulfed the entire length of the towering rocket. The sound it made was so deafening, that it could be heard many miles away. The rocket shivered and shuddered from the tremendous vibration produced by the massive engine. Spectators who were standing on a viewing platform more than a mile away from the launch site, had to cover their eyes to protect them from the blinding light emitted from the exhaust nozzle. At a full throttle, the rocket began to lift off. And within a few seconds, had broken through the sound barrier, exceeding the speed of sound, and producing a sonic boom. It continued to accelerate to speeds never achieved before. Within a few minutes, all that could be seen from the ground was the vertical trail of exhaust gases left by the spent rocket fuel. It disappeared into the upper atmosphere.

As the rocket passed through the outer atmosphere and into outer space, the capsule released the body of the rocket to fall back to earth. Suddenly, the screeching and vibration stopped, as the astronaut passed through the greatest gateway in human history.

The astronaut felt as if the capsule was standing still. Yet, he was traveling at eighteen thousand miles per hour. It was a cramped and tiny space in the capsule with barely enough room to sit perfectly still. The capsule had a small window, just inches away from his head. Through it he could see Mother Earth, spinning quietly and effortlessly beneath him. Her colors were so incredibly vivid against the black backdrop of space. All of his life he had dreamed of seeing earth from space, but never imagined that she would be as beautiful as she was. He was as fortunate a man as had ever lived, and he knew it. Tears began to well up in his eyes, as the gravity of the moment overwhelmed him. He no longer feared returning home unharmed. His thoughts were of all those who had ever imagined such a moment. He didn't think of his own personal glory anymore. He could think only of Mankind. He saw earth for the first time as finite, as a beautiful but lonely place, as a safe haven for humanity. He saw her as something to be cherished and protected, as Man's only home. He understood that there would be no second chances. He felt shame for the way Man had misused this magical place. For the first time in his life he understood Man.

In a matter of just hours, the capsule had orbited the earth several times. The astronaut had been in constant communication with the command center on the ground and began preparing for the capsule's reentry. It had been fitted with a special protective outer layer to resist the heat and friction caused by the penetration of the outer atmosphere from space. It had been calculated that the angle of reentry needed to be exact. If the angle was too shallow, the capsule will bounce off the edge of the atmosphere and catapult itself into outer space, never to return. If the angle was too steep, the capsule could accelerate to speeds that will surely kill the astronaut and destroy the tiny capsule. Reentry was the most dangerous part of the mission.

As the capsule began reentry, and left the quiet tranquility and desolation of space, it began to groan and shutter and shake violently. The friction was so great that the exterior of the capsule turned into a fireball. Traveling at thousands of feet per second, the capsule began to slow from the friction of the atmosphere. It is not unlike a rock being thrown into a pond. The water, like the atmosphere, slows the rock's momentum. At an altitude of 40,000 feet, the capsule released its parachutes in order to slow its descent even further. After a few minutes, the capsule crashed into the sea. It was within sight of the search and rescue vessel that had been sent to retrieve it from the water. The capsule's impact location had been calculated in advance of the recovery, so the astronaut and the capsule were on board the ship within minutes of impact.

The astronaut was quickly moved to a decontamination chamber where he was quarantined for a number of hours. Nobody knew if space could contaminate the human body in some way, or not. It was a necessary precaution. As he sat and waited, he was overcome by the magnitude of what has just occurred. He had come back to earth a changed man. He knew that it was quite possible that no other living creature, anywhere in the universe, had ever left the confines of their own planet. He understood that this event may not only have been a landmark achievement for mankind, but a landmark achievement for life itself. He reflected on the solitude of space and the loneliness of the tiny blue planet spinning quietly through the void since the beginning of time. He wondered of earth's past and its fate. He saw earth for the first time in his life as fragile. He had always thought of earth as an environment, but now he had seen her in her own environment. He was humbled beyond description.

Humanity's future in space seemed bright. There was speculation that he could travel to the moon, or even to distant planets. There was talk of Man living in space, of space stations, and spaceships commuting back and forth from space. Countries competed for the next great advance in space travel, and the space race had begun.

Time moved on as it always does, and years later the aging astronaut had never stopped thinking of his incredible journey to the edge of space. He often sat in a comfortable chair out on his patio, long after the sun has set, and gazed at the night sky. He dreamed of ancient star gazers, for the view had not changed since early Man came down from the safety of the woodlands and walked upright out into the open savanna. Those ancient people gazed up at the same sky, feeling the same sense of wonder. He still could not comprehend how Man has managed to get from that place to this. His awe turned to pride as the years passed. He had become a living hero. As he entered his golden years, he found himself regretting his mortality and dreamed of witnessing all he thought could come in the future. He imagined that his name and his great feat would be passed down from generation to generation. But he also feared that some future human catastrophe would ultimately end Man's space travels. He worried that space travel might become a forgotten memory, or even an unprovable historical myth. He wondered if his feat could be lost in time, lost to history.

The hopes and fears of a thousand generations, past and future, always found their way to his mind at this time of night. Staring at the heavens and sipping his cognac in the peace of his estate always sent him there. A day never passed without the weight of humanity baring down on him. He knew more than the rest of us, and understood what it meant to be human more than the rest of us. He no longer concerned himself with politics and parties. He lived mostly in his mind. And every night, he retreated to the patio with his cognac and lounger, and would fall gently asleep under the blanket of the heavens.

His spaceships would take him to the surface of the moon, and interplanetary probes would explore the surface of Mars and beyond. New technologies allow any individual on earth to communicate with any other individual on earth at their leisure. Vast quantities of information are sent back and forth at lightning speed, on invisible highways, from anywhere on the globe. Wealth continues to grow at a rate that produces literally millions of individuals across the globe living like the Kings and Emperors of old.

Meanwhile, Mankind's ancient places like Africa, are being drained of wealth and raw materials only to be abandoned, leaving tens of millions to suffer the ravages of disease and starvation. Submarines explore the deepest crevasses of the world's oceans seeking to discover the most ancient forms of life. Archaeologists dig worldwide, and uncover creatures that walked the earth millions of years before Man. They articulate elaborate theories as to why they disappeared. Scientists and scholars begin to examine the phenomenon of extinction as a real possibility for Man's fate.

Meanwhile, war is ever present. It is raging somewhere in the world at any given time. One conflict triggers another, and yet another. Every time a conflict comes to an end without a worldwide catastrophe, Man feels as though he has dodged another bullet. International organizations act as peacekeepers to intervene when conflicts last too long or spill into neighboring countries. Emergency organizations work endlessly to assist people in war torn regions. Food, fresh water, and medical supplies are flown in from all over the world to ease human suffering. With each fire that Man extinguishes, another erupts.

For many, it seems as if civilization is coming apart at the seams. For others, it feels as though Man's intelligence is finally paying off by creating wealth, lifestyles, and technologies only dreamed of in the past. Either way, Man's problems are mounting, not the least of which is waste. Astronomically amounts of waste are created every day worldwide. Tens of millions of tons of waste are being buried every year, in enormous landfills across the globe. Sometimes it is treated and reused, but it just keeps coming. The problem grows with each passing year, and an inescapable truth begins to emerge. Man is suffocating under the weight of his own populations and drowning in his own waste.

The Dump
Place: Southeast Asia
Time: Present Day

We lived there. We had been forced to make a living there. Our country is terribly overpopulated and opportunities are hard to come by. Most of the population scratched out a living any way they could. Most of us cannot read or write well or at all. We never had the luxury of schooling. The rich are very rich, but we are very poor. My wife and I have two children, a little girl who is seven and my boy who is ten. Well I say my wife but we were never married. You need money to get married. We don't have money and we are the only family either of us have ever known. We have been together since we were fifteen years old. Life is hard, but we take care of each other just like the rich people do. The only difference between us and them is they have money and we don't. We do the best we can.

My family lived on the edge of the largest garbage dump on the island. We had made a shelter that protected us from the wind and the rains. It was made out of sheet metal, wire, and scraps of plywood. It was big enough for all of us to cook, eat, and sleep in. It was more than a lot of the people had. I once had a job in construction for a couple of months and learned how to build. That hut has stood in even the strongest winds. It wasn't much, but it is all we had. As soon as dawn came, all of us headed out to the sight on the dump where the new loads of garbage were brought the day before. We did this every day. It was our routine. We always tried to get there first, ahead of everyone else. I had never counted everybody who lives here, but if I had to guess, I would say there is about a hundred or so. You had to be first to find the best stuff, meaning the stuff that we could sell. Aluminum cans and copper wire are really what we were all looking for mostly. When you collected enough of either, you could take them to the recycling center on the far end of the dump for money. Although the garbage company took as much of those things out of the garbage as they could before it even went to the dump, they did miss a lot. One week alone I sold eleven dollars worth of aluminum to the recycling center. Some weeks were better than others. It was a day to day existence there. I am sure it still is.

Our people there got sick a lot with coughing, and infected sores on their feet and hands. Many died without any medicine treatment or even clean bandages. Some were buried right in the dump. Others were taken to the street in front of the dump where the authorities would pick them up and dispose of them. I prayed every day that this would not be my children's fate. It would have been all right if I died in the dump, but not my children. If I could only save enough to move into a tenement in the city and find a job, my children would have a chance. But I felt I couldn't protect them in the city like I could there. In the city there is much crime, along with violence and abuse. Our choices were never easy. I saw the helplessness in my wife's face. I reassured her whenever I could and reminded her that better days were ahead for us. She listened and wanted desperately to believe me. But our day to day reality told her otherwise. Her tears had all but dried up a long time before. Mine had too. We felt as though we have been forgotten by the world. I know I had made mistakes throughout my life and sometimes felt that was why we ended up in that miserable place. Maybe that was so, maybe not.

As I approached the loads of garbage that were brought in the day before I couldn't believe my eyes. Under a mattress I saw a thick rubber coated copper wire. It looked to be almost an inch thick. I paused for a second to see if any of the other people saw it too. But nobody seemed to be looking in this direction. I tried to contain my excitement and climbed slowly over to the mattress. We had a lot of false alarms on the dump. You thought you may have found something but it turned out to be something else or nothing at all. I lifted the corner of the mattress and the most incredible sight I had ever seen stared back at me. I called out to my wife and children to hurry. They could hear it in my voice and move quickly to my side. We surrounded the mattress because sometimes we have to fight for what we find. The look on our faces must have been something to see. We all took a gasp of air and sighed together as if it were rehearsed. We were standing over a pile of copper wire that could feed us for a month. The wire was an inch thick in pieces between about six and twelve inches in length. There had to be at least a hundred or so pieces. The garbage company had somehow missed it. We looked at each other and knew exactly what to do. I stayed with our precious find and began collecting the pieces of wire so they were all within arms reach. I kept the mattress over the wire as to hide it from the others. My wife and children quickly collected bags and cloth to carry the wire. As each of them found something that would hold the weight, they brought it to me. I filled the bags with the wire. My mind was racing. We would not have had a second chance to return to that spot if we couldn't take it all with us in one load. We had tried to hide what we couldn't carry before, but it never worked. Someone always saw you and the rest was never there when you came back. I organized the loads so that they were lighter for the children, a little heavier for my wife, and the heaviest for me. I was able to wrap up all the copper wire that we found. Then we had to get it off the dump.

We were about five hundred yards away from where we could exit the dump near the recycling center. It was only five hundred yards, but it is over the top of the garbage dump. You can't just run there because the surface of the dump is always shifting and unstable and the copper was heavy. We had to use caution as always or one of us would get badly cut or even break a leg on the debris. Together we moved slowly across the dump. We would never be more that a few feet away from each another. The threat of having to fight for our find was real. By that time, nearly everyone on this section of the dump was watching us. Luck was with us that day because they all hurried to the place we had found the wire and began digging. But we had gotten all of it and by the time they figured that out we were too far away for them to catch us. It probably took us four hours to walk five hundred yards across the dump. We were exhausted and had cuts on our legs, but it didn't matter. We were headed for the biggest payday of all our years on the dump. Five years we spent on the dump to be exact.

By then it was early afternoon when we arrived at the entrance to the recycling center. We knew the man at the window and he nodded when he saw us. That meant that it was all right to come in. We dragged our loads directly to the giant scale just inside the doorway. The man's eyes lit up when he saw what we were carrying. He smiled slightly as if to acknowledge our joy and relief in owning a load of such value. He reminded us that copper of that thickness was valuable, but that he would have to subtract 2 percent from the weight to account for the rubber. I agreed. Our eyes were fixed on the scale's dial as the last piece of copper was piled on. I reached for my wife's hand just as the dial settled in on three hundred twenty four pounds. I turned and saw a sight I thought I would never see again. There were tears streaming down my wife's face. In fact, we all had tears streaming down our faces. We stood in silence as the man announced that the total weight minus the rubber was three hundred seventeen and one half pounds. At seventy-nine cents per pound, he said he owed us two hundred fifty dollars and eighty-two cents. It was as if time had stood still. We were all silent and trembling.

The man walked over to the office and disappeared through the doorway. A few minutes later he emerged with the money in his hand and a big smile on his face. I could barely lift my head to meet his eyes as I reached for the money. I was overwhelmed with emotion. He knew like we knew, that the money he just handed me was our ticket out of that wretched place. That was our chance to live with a dignity that we had never known before. The four of us immediately embraced each other and sobbed together in what seemed like eternity. An angel had visited us that day. It was a day that none of us would ever forget. We left there together that afternoon, all hand in hand, as quiet as can be. No one said a word. We all knew where we were headed. We were headed to the city, never to return to our shack on the edge of the dump. For the first time in our lives, we had hope. Until now, we had never spoken of that time in our life, not to anyone, not even to each other.

Man's population explosion continues unabated into the twenty first century, and the impact on the environment is mounting. In the populated areas throughout the globe nearly everything is completely contaminated. Food and water need to be treated, essentially decontaminated, prior to consumption. Topsoil is eroding, as over farming relentlessly exhausts the soil. Acid rain falls on wild areas as Man's pollution is carried on the winds to distant places. Fishing grounds in fresh and salt water are either fished out, declining, or contaminated. Coral reefs, considered by all as the jewel of the seas and foundation of marine ecosystems, are dying.

The great forests of the world are vanishing as well. Thousands of square miles of woodlands are being destroyed every year on the South American continent alone. And disappearing along with those wild areas are all the creatures living there. Big and small, reptile or insect or mammal, they all have at least one thing in common with Man. They, like Man, have nowhere else to go. Unlike the nomads of the African savanna two hundred thousand years before, who could always relocate, Modern Man no longer has that option. And as a result, countless species are disappearing at a rate not seen since the earth's last great mass extinction. Man is simply decimating the animal populations across the globe because of his burgeoning population. Nothing has remained untouched and the world's ecosystems are in dire straits. But before Man has ended his reign on earth, he will see the day that all of the carnivores that harassed him so relentlessly in those early days will have been completely extinguished.

Extinction
Place: Planet Earth
Time: Present Day

—Press Release
HABITAT LOSS SPELLS TROUBLE FOR
THE INDIAN TIGER
January

The worlds most respected scientific organization stated Thursday at an international convention on wildlife management that the Indian tiger is nearing extinction. There is an estimated 1300 Indian Tigers remaining in the wild. Leading scientists expect that the odds of their population recovering from such a low number of individuals is 'highly unlikely'. Scientists cited that habitat loss was a major contributor to the tigers' decline. The tiger's habitat has plummeted in size by 40% in the last decade alone. 'But this phenomenon is not exclusive to the tiger' they stated, 'Most of the worlds animals are suffering a severe loss of critical living space.'

The Indian Tiger made headlines last month when a major American zoo announced yet another failed attempt at reproducing an offspring in captivity. The zoo's director said back in December "We have lost three cubs in the last four years, and our tigers are in deteriorating health. We have brought in specialists from all over the world without success. The tigers are a huge attraction for our patrons that generates much needed money for the zoo's operating costs. I fear that the loss of our tigers could put the zoo itself in financial jeopardy."

The recent media attention on the tigers' plight has uncovered a larger global situation and some staggering statistics. For example, It is estimated that 80% of the worlds natural forests have already been destroyed due to unregulated logging, clearing land for agricultural use, and urban expansion. When asked about it, a lobbyist for the logging industry stated "Our operations are extremely sensitive to the environment." That may be true, but it is estimated that 70% of the earths land-based animal and plant life resides in those woodlands. This could have an irreversible impact on wildlife, as the growing number of animals making the endangered species list suggests.

In North America, there are currently more than 400 animals on the endangered species list. Worldwide, the number of endangered animals exceeds one thousand. Large mammals that make the list are the right whale, blue whale, fin whale, and the African and Asian Elephant. Primates on the list include the hybrid spider monkey, the golden lion tamarin, and of course the mighty gorilla. The mountain gorilla numbers are below 700 individuals worldwide. The tiger is not the only carnivore facing extinction either. Included on the list are the following: The red wolf, three species of leopards, Asiatic Cheetah, Florida cougar, Iberian lynx, Texas ocelot, giant panda, lesser panda, and the marine otter. And if the endangered list is accurate, then there are more than one thousand more animals in trouble. In a recent interview, a local developer stated, 'The environmentalists are over reacting, they are more concerned about animals than people.' Regardless of varying opinions on animal management, all agree that extinction is permanent. 'There is a point at which a dwindling population cannot resist the gravitational pull of extinction. There is a point of no return,' stated a leading scientific journal. 'There have been more extinctions in the last century than at any time since the end of the last ice age.'

Many believe that the growing number of extinctions is just a symptom of an even greater problem. The human population explosion over the last century appears to have significantly contributed to the shrinking animal habitats worldwide. There seems to be no debate on that issue. The human population has tripled since 1900. Most of that growth happened in the last 50 years from impoverished areas such as Africa and Southeast Asia. Africa's population alone has tripled since 1960. Recent figures show that the population is growing by 78 million individuals every year and is quickly approaching a total worldwide population of seven billion. Third world countries are worse off, as some are experiencing complete ecological collapse. Woodlands are being decimated and used for fuel. Endangered animals are being hunted for food and poached for hides and ivory. International efforts to contain illegal trade of animal goods have been difficult and frustrating.

'Deforestation leads to ecological collapse, and once that process starts it is almost impossible to stop', said a leading official. 'It is a runaway problem which needs to be addressed'. It is estimated that millions of people in third world countries are currently suffering from starvation, due in part, to deforestation. International relief efforts are ongoing.

Shortly after the conference convened Thursday, scientists urged tiger management officials to renew efforts to protect the tigers remaining habitats. 'It will be a sad day for humanity if this majestic animal disappears forever. How will we explain to our grandchildren that we let the tiger slip away?'

The ecological devastation from Man's exploding population is now so vast, that its effects can be seen from space. Man tries to save some areas as the global situation worsens, but ultimately his attempts to slow or reverse the damage will be in vain. Animals and plants are being squeezed out of existence, but they are not the only living things that are disappearing.

Still, in existence in the most remote and forgotten places on earth, are remnants of Ancient Man. Surviving against all odds, these isolated and tiny populations of nomads and hunter-gatherers live as they did thousands of years before. They are the last remaining members of humanity's distant past. They live in places like the Central Asian plateau, the South American and southeast Asian jungle, southern Africa, and in the interior of Australia. They hunt in packs with primitive weapons as commercial airliners roar overhead. They fish with bow and arrow as their waterways are being contaminated by toxins carried on the winds from far away. They follow herds of oxen and goat and cattle while satellites photograph their lands from space. They live in the deep jungles and listen to the distant rumbling of loggers eating away their homes. Their culture and traditions have been handed down by word of mouth from one generation to the next over thousands of years. But their days are numbered. They will soon become just a memory as Man's industrial world devours their ancestral lands.

Meanwhile, the industrialized populations that are driving trade, growth, and invention, are faring very well. The life expectancy for humans in industrialized nations skyrockets to nearly eighty years. Many are living well into their nineties and some more than one hundred years. Medical treatment transplants hearts, livers, lungs, and kidneys. Severed legs and arms are successfully reattached, and antibiotic technology kills microscopic evils that have plagued Man since the beginning of time. This is the place Man has dreamed he would find. This is the place he wanted to travel to so many years ago.

Disappearing Cultures
Place: Global Corporate Headquarters
CEO's Office
Time: Present Day

'Margaret?'
'Yes sir, can I help you?'
'Can you have my flight pushed back one hour?'
'Certainly sir, I will notify your pilot immediately. Do you still wish to arrive in London this evening?'
'Yes I do.'
'Can I do anything else for you?'
'No Margaret, thank you.'

I wish there were more time in the day. The stress is really starting to get to me. My morning workouts have been mildly productive at best and the late dinner meetings are wearing me out. My workload is immense, having to oversee operations in twenty-six countries. But the traveling I don't mind at all, because our new corporate jet is amazing. It can cruise just above forty thousand feet and at speeds of more than four hundred miles per hour. It has a maximum range of thirty-one hundred nautical miles and is very comfortable. It is brand new on the market, and the company just purchased the first nine production units. I fly to Paris this afternoon for a meeting and then on to London. As it looks now I won't arrive in London until quite late. I will need to email the director of our UK operations to let him know I will be delayed. He should have the presentation for tomorrow in good order. I have no worries there. He is a good man.

I am delayed this morning because of an impromptu video conference with our South American public relations officer. Margaret told me that he was in a near panic last night when he called. Apparently, he had sent numerous emails to me over the last few days. I just have not been able to answer all the emails I receive. From just yesterday alone I received ninety-seven emails. I really need to have human resources hire an assistant for Margaret just to handle emails. It is becoming a problem. Anyway, our South American office has a situation down there with the local officials. As soon as I heard that, I assumed that our operations are being held up because some official down there has his hand out. They are always looking for hand outs in that part of the world. This is exactly why these people still live in the dark ages. There are certain ways to conduct business, and any deviation from that always create problems. These people don't understand procedure, or chain of command. They don't understand the basics.

The issue is some war, or skirmish, or something that has halted construction of phase II of our energy project. Which of course is nothing new. It has happened at least twice before, mainly because that particular operation is in one of the most godforsaken places on earth, the South American jungle. But, we go where the business is, and that's it. It is just part of managing a global corporation. Either way, I cannot afford to have any more delays in construction.

Apparently, the local officials down there have been trying to extract armed drug lords from government lands where they have set up shop manufacturing illegal drugs. And in the process of hunting them down, a number of indigenous tribesmen have been caught in the crossfire and killed. I understand that the population of these tribesmen has been shrinking for years and that these recent fatalities are throwing up red flags everywhere. Notwithstanding the fact that governments around the world have joined forces to put an end to illegal international drug trafficking. In addition, the government land where all this is happening is in fact the same land our corporation has leased from their government for the energy operation. This is a volatile issue and I have no desire to position my company on the wrong side of public opinion. We have paid good money, and a lot of it, to lease the property. Our investment will not be compromised any further under my watch. I'll guarantee you that.

Environmental organizations, human rights groups, and the rest of them are down there, right now. The international media will pick it up by tomorrow morning. I'm sure. We will have to move quickly to a damage control mode, again. Our damage control apparatus is very effective, but quite costly as well. Our stockholders always have an issue with expenditures related to damage control. It is becoming an incessant problem and the responsibility always ends up with me. I have news for you though, my South American public relations officer will be looking for work next month. I need someone there who can handle these things before they get blown out of proportion.

I will need to call our VP of Media Relations and get started on an ad campaign to bolster our position in public opinion. It is essential that we continue to be perceived as a concerned and environmentally sensitive corporation. Our company has spent tens of millions of dollars and many years constructing our brand image. It was I who initially implemented that program. Nobody knows better than I, that perception is reality.

Maybe we can announce the construction of a new medical clinic to provide free medical care to the natives down there. With health care costs going through the roof, 'free' medicine always sounds good. Maybe even set up a job clinic to help teach the locals useful job skills. We'll put them to work, so they can provide for their families in a more civilized way. I mean, for gods sake, these people live in the jungle and have nothing. They could be of great assistance in the construction phase. Well, in support positions I mean. Who knows the jungle better than they do? We can also build a school for the kids, with free books and pencils. Oh, this is good. We'll send our media team to shoot live video of those little kids, filing into a new school with new uniforms and big smiles on their faces. I could have a field day with this. We will donate, say, one million dollars to the government there to assist in their efforts to rid themselves of the drug lords. That will produce a lot of positive press internationally and give us some political currency to spend with local officials.

We will then start a smear campaign against illegal logging. They will make a great scape goat to take any pressure off of us. The loggers are destroying the environment down there anyhow. They are the real problem. They are clear-cutting the jungle where these poor people live. They are the problem, and you know what, we are the solution.

We'll give them jobs and opportunity, schools and a medical clinic. We'll look like heroes.

My job isn't easy. It never is. The responsibility falls on my shoulders, and for that service I am compensated very well. And you know what? I deserve it. I have made a lot of sacrifices for this job. I hardly see my kids anymore, and my wife probably wouldn't recognize me if she saw me. But she has her own chauffeur and lives in an enormous palace on the ocean. She, more than anyone, has absolutely nothing to complain about.

If we make our numbers this year, I will make my bonus. It won't be as big as last year, but it will be big enough. Twenty-eight million dollars and another forty thousand shares of common stock will be my pay off when the numbers come in. Three more years. Only three more years, and I'll have enough to retire. It's not bad for a poor kid from New Jersey. Life is good.

Extinctions on earth are an undeniable truth. At some point in time, Mankind will be no more. When it happens and how it happens, are the only matters left to debate. There is one notable difference between Mankind and all the other species on earth. And that is, that human beings are earths first species that is aware of the phenomenon of extinction. It is in that awareness where humanity's only hope of delaying the inevitable lies. But only time will tell if future generations of Man will still possess that awareness.

Remember, when societies and civilizations collapse, knowledge is lost. The greater the calamity, the greater the loss. And the more sophisticated the technology, the easier it is to lose. It is certainly within the realm of possibility that ten thousand years from now humanity will not remember a time when a spaceship carried a man to the moon. Could an ancient Egyptian ever imagine a time in the future when Egypt forgot how to build a pyramid?

So, is there an extinction event in Man's future in the form of a rogue asteroid or a massive volcanic event? Maybe. Or will Man meet his end after enduring a series of calamities ignited by a world war fought over religion or vanishing resources? Many would say that these are the greatest possibilities.

But the one condition which always triggers a series of catastrophic events, for any species, Man or beast, is a runaway population. And runaway populations, nearly always result in a mass die-off. This could be the scenario most likely to propel humanity into an irreversible decline. Based on the current rate of growth, Mankind appears to be barreling toward a worldwide population collapse. If so, it could be humanity's most dire predicament since wandering the African savanna two hundred thousand years ago.

978-0-595-47111-9
0-595-47111-0

Lightning Source UK Ltd.
Milton Keynes UK
28 June 2010

156228UK00001B/91/A